A Mansion in the Sky
And Other Short Stories

Modern Middle East
Literatures in Translation Series

A Mansion in the Sky
And Other Short Stories

Goli Taraghi

Introduction and Translation

by

Faridoun Farrokh

Center for Middle Eastern Studies
University of Texas at Austin

Library of Congress Catalogue Card Number: 2003111753
ISBN: 0-292-70226-4

Printed in the United States of America

Cover design: Diane Watts

Series editor: Annes McCann-Baker

Acknowledgments

Translators are forever indebted to their original authors, who have inspired and given impetus to their undertakings. This case is no exception, considering the extraordinary generosity that Goli Taraghi has accorded me by entrusting her work to me for the purpose of this translation, as well as giving me guidance where needed and latitude where possible.

Among colleagues and friends who have taken an interest in this work, I mention only M.R. Ghanoonparvar and will let him represent all the others who have given me invaluable counsel and assistance in bringing this project to fruition. Needless to say, I am immeasurably thankful to Annes McCann-Baker, Editor of the Center for Middle Eastern Studies at The University of Texas at Austin, and her colleagues who saw value in my rough-hewn work and gave it the necessary polish for exposure to public view.

As arbiters of taste in contemporary English idiom, Cindy and Lara, my wife and daughter respectively, have embossed their seal of approval on this work. I thank them for it.

Faridoun Farrokh

Introduction

In the last twenty years or so of Iran's Pahlavi regime, Goli Taraghi emerged as a member of a relatively small group of women in Iran who were active in writing fiction and were able to achieve recognition in this endeavor. Aside from Simin Daneshvar and the widespread popularity of her novel *Savushun*, few other women writers surpassed Taraghi's success and reputation, despite the fact that she was never a prolific writer. Taraghi was born and raised in Tehran, the daughter of the noted publisher and editor Lotfollah Taraghi. She received a baccalaureate in philosophy from Drake University in Iowa and a master's degree in sociology from the University of Tehran. The collection of her short stories, *Man ham Che Guevara hastam* (A Che Guevara in My Own Right), and a loosely structured novel, *Khab-e Zemestani* (Winter Sleep), published respectively in 1969 and 1973, were fairly popular and elicited favorable commentary from the critical establishment in Iran.

Taraghi writes in a style that is unique and entirely her own. She avoids sensational experimentation and wild departures from the mainstream techniques of story-telling, and yet she gives freshness and vigor to her artistic vision by creating characters who ring true because they are realistically and sensitively conceived. It is true, however, that Taraghi's characters do not exhibit much social range and psychological variety. In the stories Taraghi wrote before 1980, there is a marked absence of women and, for that matter, romantic interest. A typical character in her early fiction is the male urban dweller, more specifically, a resident of Tehran, who is almost always literate and in a few cases even erudite with a touch of pedantry. In terms of social standing, these characters are predominantly from the lower scales of the middle class. They are very much the products of contemporary Iran: although they experience the joys and sorrows universal to humanity, they cannot be imagined in any dimension other than the Iranian framework constructed for them by Taraghi. Surprisingly, few if any of them are fashioned after the members of her immediate circle of acquaintance or the vast coterie of very interesting, even intriguing, individuals she associated with during the years she lived in Iran.

Though technically male, the characters in Taraghi's pre-revolution fiction seem to have been emasculated by the environment in which they exist. As such, the question of gender becomes subordinate to the message implanted in the subtext of her stories, which is, more often than not, a tacit condemnation of the parvenu culture and value system promulgated by the dominant social and political order. In the emotional dilapidation and defective masculinity of her characters, Taraghi appears to imply the cultural entropy and moral drift of the status quo. To some extent, Taraghi's ambivalence about her artistic identity may be due to her desire to put an aesthetic distance between herself and the characters that populate her fiction. This is not to say, however, that she is hesitant to assert the potency of her imagination or to exercise her prerogative to write as a woman. For all the years she lived in Tehran and within the family compound, in a milieu unquestionably patriarchal and male-dominated, it is remarkable that Taraghi succeeded in sustaining her creativity by conjuring up male characters whose masculinity is a mere biological detail and of no consequence in the development of the narrative.

In the absence of gender as an impetus to drive the plot, Taraghi uses irony to create dramatic tension and sustain reader interest. Irony in Taraghi's fiction is generally effected through the distortions intrinsic to the parallax view she gives of her characters. The nominal maleness of the men in her stories is an example of such distortion. These men are basically parodies of themselves and, to be understood by the reader, they have to be "reconstructed," a term Wayne C. Booth uses in connection with the "slight distortion" of parody and identifies as the mechanism by which parody communicates "some kind of argument or message." The reason, according to Booth, is that "ironic reconstruction never yields only a single, literal message, because the action of choosing irony and all of its consequences remains part of what is communicated" (137). That is why the pathetic nature of Taraghi's characters is not merely a caricaturing of their archetype, but also a ridiculing of the society that has engendered them. As readers, we find ourselves implicated in the social environment that envelopes the characters. We share vicariously their experiences, although we are exempt from actually identifying with them.

To maintain the focus on the emotional state of the characters, Taraghi avoids melodrama and keeps external action to a minimum. The action in *Winter Sleep*, for example, is entirely internal. It depicts the interactive relationship among a handful of men who associate with one another for no apparent reason other than perhaps the fact that they are all minor officials of a company or government agency. They are just used to one another, and none has the initiative to break out and seek more meaningful liaisons outside the peer group. They all seem to resent one another in some degree and, most of all, the person or persons who have arrogated to themselves the leadership position in the relationship. Still, out of sheer emotional lethargy they remain submissive to the perceived leader. In *Winter Sleep* nothing dramatic or consequential happens. There is no friction, conflict, or outward violence to punctuate the stream of the narrator's consciousness. In the introduction to her translation of the novel, Francine Mahak notes that the picture [Taraghi] presents in *Winter Sleep* is "deceptively simple, and yet we see the tragedy of the individual's stagnation within the empty shell of his uprooted culture" (Taraqqi vii). In addition to this "stagnation" running as a thread through Taraghi's stories, the narratives are also held together by an ominous sense of an impending doom, an expectation of internal collapse, an implosion to decimate the group and leave its members ravaged and disoriented. That event in *Winter Sleep* is the sudden and unexpected death of the novel's central character and with it the failure of a real-estate investment deal he was negotiating on behalf of the group.

The way these characters behave and enunciate their values and convictions sets them apart from the reader, further deepening the parodic distortion. Thus, as Booth points out, "the most evident purpose of the irony is achieved when unacceptable statements or arguments or judgments have been reconstructed into what the author believes and expects us to believe with him" (137).

Taraghi's motive for such a camouflaging stratagem may be sought in the social conditions under which she lived and wrote. Even as late as the 1960s, most criticism of women's literary endeavors was "rife with misconceptions [and] sexually biased assumptions," writes Farzaneh Milani. "One frequent manifestation of such limiting criticism," she continues, "is excessive attention to sensual and erotic themes. Masculine criticism operating according to masculine conceptions and values concentrates on this one aspect and, by its very superficiality, trivializes the work it examines" (117-118).

Mary DeShazer identifies this circumstance as a "double bind." According to her, the situation in which women writers such as Taraghi find themselves is essentially "a quest for both personal and poetic identity within a society and a literary tradition that view 'woman' and 'poet' as mutually exclusive terms." She concludes that in a tradition that habitually eschews the notion of woman-writer, "this struggle causes fragmentation; the woman-poet asserts 'I am,' but follows her statement of identity with a question mark as often as an exclamation" (4).

In her later writing, especially after the fall of the Pahlavi regime and her departure from Iran, Taraghi meticulously and inexorably took down the wall that insulated her from her work. As a result, her post-revolutionary fiction, of which the present collection is a prime example, has become increasingly autobiographical. In these works she delves into the recesses of her memory for details, which she then reconfigures in intricate patterns of plot and character development, eliciting a much more emotive response form the reader. The change is due not so much to a process of maturing as to the experience of life in exile. In fact, several of Taraghi's new stories deal with the acculturation process and the heartbreak of uprooting and displacement.

In this collection, the first four stories share the common theme of pubescent sexual and emotional awakening. Each story, told from the viewpoint of a young girl (and not necessarily the same one), reflects the agonizing uncertainties, obsessions, and intertwining of new, conflicting feelings and urges characteristic of early adolescence. However, these stories, and the ones that follow on the theme of exile, are not mere reflections of autobiographical experience and expressions of private feelings. The sequencing and foregrounding of episodes in these works underline the ambivalence of the position of women in the social context of the narrative and suggest a strain of feminist protest in the fabric of each story. Similar to her previous work, Taraghi structures her plots within the framework of a patriarchal society. As Marilyn French points out, in a world for the most part patriarchal, "feminist literature necessarily depicts patriarchy." However, as she contends, this tendency "does not underwrite its standards" (68). This is manifestly true of Taraghi's fiction. To prevent her work from becoming polemical, and thus subjugating its aesthetics to ideology, Taraghi avoids outright condemnations of her male-dominated milieu. She eschews an expression of impatience and frustration with the oppressive nature of a patriarchal world in general. Rather, she allows the nuances in the narrative flux to lead the reader to the intended conclusion. In the words of Marilyn French, "[i]n a work with feminist perspective, the narrational point of view, the point of view lying behind the characters and events, penetrates, demystifies, and challenges patriarchal ideologies" (68). For example, in "Grandma's House," we learn through flashbacks that the uncle of the protagonist, having been jilted by his wife, has gone berserk. The picture of the uncle is not the romanticized image of the lover in agony for the loss of the beloved, but that of a man who has had a prized possession taken away from him. The reasons for the wife's desertion are not specified, but some hints suggest undue jealousy and possessiveness on the part of the husband. It is against this background that we learn the woman was justified in leaving her husband. In portraying female experience, as French posits, "feminist art also portrays men, showing them as they impinge upon women or as they appear to women. . . What men are in themselves or for other men may contradict what they are for women" (71). Accordingly, the portrait of the deserted uncle, depicted by the narrator, a pubescent girl, emerges as pathetic, almost grotesque, and unworthy of compassion.

Among the stories, "The Maid" is an anomaly. Unlike other stories in the collection, this one has a narrator who stays almost totally out of the focus of events and has no role in the unfolding of the plot. The antagonist is a maid, a young woman of the lower classes, who behaves enigmatically when she is hired into the service of an upper-class household. In the course of the story, Taraghi explores class relations and raises questions on the issues of personal conduct and economic determinism.

The next story, "A Mansion in the Sky," is typical of Taraghi's recent fiction which reflects her experience in exile within the context of a feminist perspective. The story revolves around an Iranian dowager who is caught in the cataclysm of sweeping change brought about by her children and their selfish pursuits. Her son auctions off her house and belongings so he can live abroad on the proceeds, far from the turbulence of post-revolutionary Tehran in the grips of the Iran-Iraq war. Thereafter, the old woman is passed back and forth between her son and daughter, who gradually come to regard her as a mere nuisance. In its basic simplicity, "The Mansion" has a complex infrastructure. It reveals the intricate web of Iranian cultural norms that render the woman impotent, both emotionally and legally, in the exertion of her will or preferences.

The final story in this volume, "The Bizarre Comportment of Mr. Alpha in Exile" may be considered the reflection of Taraghi's earliest experience as an emigrée. She wrote it during the first few months of her residence in Paris. Very much like Taraghi's other work, the story features a man as the main character. Mr. Alpha, a former history teacher in a girls' secondary school in Tehran, appears to have had no contact with the world outside his professional associations before his removal to Paris. He appears socially limited and inept. Consequently, his experience of living in Paris and the concomitant cultural shock is excruciating for him. We discover that he came to Paris in the early days of the revolution after a rock-throwing incident in which he received a severe blow to his head and a more severe one to his ego. To add insult to injury, some unidentified students singled him out as an object of their anti-establishment fury by serving him a mock death warrant. Mr. Alpha, who considers himself a dedicated teacher and a man of refined sensibility, took these events very much to heart and in a tantrum-like fit of anger decided to leave the country, despite the fact that he was deeply and, for all intents and purposes, platonically, involved in a liaison with a physical education teacher who happened to be the wife of a childhood friend. Painstakingly, in depicting the character of Mr. Alpha, Taraghi delineates the stereotype of the Iranian middle-class intellectual: passive, detached, self-absorbed, and genuinely baffled by the turn of events that have caused him inconvenience and distress. He is clearly vapid and ineffectual, suggesting that the suffering he has received at the hands of others, including a harsh, martinet father, is generally the result of his own inanity and lack of moral resolve. He is the kind of person that can be victimized and exploited but never martyred.

These stories indicate novel aspects of Taraghi's development as a writer and deserve closer and more extensive scrutiny. As a whole, Goli Taraghi's recent work demonstrates a trend in which she views her creative self unflinchingly as feminine and is more willing to focus her work on her gender-related experiences. Arguably, Taraghi's work has become richer and more poignant as a result of this transformation, and perhaps more polemical and intellectually contentious.

ABOUT THE TEXT

This translation is based on the original Persian text of *Khaterat-e Parakandeh: Majmu'eh-ye Qesseh*, published by Intisharat-i Bagh-i Ayinah, Tehran, 1371/1993.

WORKS CITED

Booth, Wayne C. *A Rhetoric of Irony*. Chicago: University of Chicago Press, 1997.

DeShazer, Mary K., ed. *Inspiring Woman: Reimagining the Muse*. New York: Pergamon Press, 1986.

French, Marilyn. "Is There a Feminist Aesthetic?" *Aesthetics in Feminist Perspective.* Eds. Hilde Hein and Carolyn Korsmeyer. Bloomington: Indiana University Press, 1993.

Milani, Farzaneh. "Love and Sexuality in the Poetry of Forough Farrokhzad: A Reconsideration." *Iranian Studies.* Volume XV, 1982, Nos. 1-4, 117-128.

Taraqqi, Goli. *Winter Sleep.* Trans. Francine Mahak. Costa Mesa, California: Mazda Publishers, 1994.

The Shemiran Bus

Number 70 bus pulls away from the curb before we get to it. My little girl runs a little ways after it, but before getting to the corner loses hope and stops. We wait for the next bus.

An unexpected snow is falling. The air is full of a translucent mist, and a pleasant silence has replaced the usual hubbub of the city. Everywhere is white and calm. Passers-by disappear in the mist like apparitions, and only outlines of trees and houses are distinguishable. In the eight years we have been here in Paris, this is the first really heavy snow we have seen.

"Angels are house cleaning," I hear the voice of my grandmother at the back of my head. "They're dusting the clouds and sweeping the carpets of the sky."

I am put in mind of Tehran in winter, dominated by the tall, snow-clad Alborz peak underneath the turquoise-blue skies, the bare, sleeping trees in the far end of our garden, dreaming of the return of migrating birds.

In my childhood, snowy days had no end . . . Saturday, Sunday, Monday. I counted the days . . . Tuesday, Wednesday, Thursday, and the snow continued to fall. Ten centimeters, twenty centimeters, half a meter, to the point that snow would block doors and the schools would close for a whole week.

What a joy! What an unbelievable good fortune! A whole week of staying in bed in the mornings and playing with all those girls and boys, my cousins all, in the alley. A week without the bother of having to face the assistant principal or encountering that sourpuss of a math teacher, not having to read from the *Holy Precepts* book or the Koran, or do writing exercises. A week of not having to memorize those interminable, stupid poems or do calligraphy practice with reed pens and black ink. Free from the clutches of lessons and school. Seven glorious days of fun and games!

It was such a treat for us kids when we had company and the snow closed the streets. The guests stayed over, two, three nights at a time. Frequent guests in our house included:

—My scrawny, tenderhearted grandmother who was always at prayer, asking God to give us happiness, health and wealth.

—Bibi Jan, my mother's old aunt, hard of hearing and senile, who confused me with my brother, my brother with my cousin, my cousin with the neighbor's kid and the neighbor's kid with me.

—My favorite, Aunt Azar, whose brats noisily played leap-frog in the hallway and climbed on everything in sight and screamed like a bunch of wild monkeys as they slid down the banister.

—My Uncle Ahmad Khan, the gentlest and the most tenderhearted dentist in the world, who could not bring himself to extract a tooth, and his eyes misted every time he saw one of the kids crying.

—Big Uncle, the artillery officer, who was deathly scared of horses and guns and upon arrival would get out of his uniform, put on an apron, and get busy in the kitchen making delicious fruit preserves or knitting colorful woolen pullovers.

—And, last but not least, the fat and easy-going Tooba Khanum, who knew a wealth of bizarre stories and was into cultism and witchcraft and sometimes played magic tricks for us.

All these people stayed in our house until the snow melted and streets became passable. I cherished those crowded rooms spread wall to wall with blankets and bedding. There were tables everywhere, covered with all kinds of snacks, tankards of refreshments, bowls full of pomegranate seed, dishes of candy, and the delicious baklava, my mother's specialty.

It felt so good when all the rooms, hallways, and parlors were redolent with a thousand aromas arising from every corner of the house: the pungent smell of tobacco from my grandmother's water pipe, Bibi Jan's herbal tea, the fragrance of saffron being spread over the rice along with rose water and caraway seeds and cinnamon, the smell of onions frying in the pan and strips of lamb grilled to a crisp on hot coals.

I loved to be lulled to sleep by the drone of adult sounds coming from other rooms—Little Uncle strumming on the stringed *tar* and Aunt Azar sweetly humming, my mother's slippers clacking on the staircase. Sometimes I would wake up in the middle of the night and feel the big folks still up and about, lights on and the kitchen in full swing. I would drift off again in a sleep as light and airy as the whimsical flight of a balloon.

This evening the fall of the snow has evoked a similar childish thrill in me. My little girl is also excited. She dances round and round and hurls snowballs at no targets in particular. She ambles along the street, anxiously waiting for another bus to arrive. Her restlessness reminds me of my own little palpitating heart when every day after school I waited at the bus stop counting seconds in anticipation of seeing my friend, Aziz Agha.

I lift my face up to the sky and open my mouth to catch the drifting flakes of snow. To me, they have a delicious taste and a pleasant smell. It is as if countless petals of jasmine are falling from heaven. I feel as if I am levitating and floating in the air, as if I am in a glass bubble and a hidden breath sucks me back to the past.

I see myself when I was ten, waiting for the Shemiran bus at an intersection near school. Our new house is way out of town behind the hills and in the middle of an empty subdivision. There are no houses around ours. Sometimes at night, we could hear the coyotes. My mother gets scared. So does Hassan Agha, the cook, who spreads his bedding next to my father's bedroom door for protection. I like the desolate locations of our house. I am not scared of the water reservoir and the pool that are full of frogs and tadpoles in the summer, or the dark, malevolent-looking shadows cast by the trees. At the end of the garden I have erected a makeshift tent with a discarded bed sheet. No one can find me there. I hide my snacks under a brick and bury the assignment on which I have made failing grades so my mother won't see them. The poplars are my companions and each has a name of its own. The taller ones are boys. When I get back from school, I throw down my satchel and run to the end of the garden. I report my daily activities to the trees, showing them my schoolwork and reading to them from the textbook. Some of them are dumb and start yawning with boredom. Some are jealous and mean and purposely ignore my performance. I kiss the ones that are friendly and stick small pieces of gum behind their leaves. Those who have said nasty things behind my back are punished and their branches are tied together with rope.

On the bus, it takes more than an hour to get to Firoozkuhi School. My older brother can go by himself, but I have to be escorted to school by Hassan Agha. However, he gives me free rein on the way, because if he says a word to my mother I can get him in serious trouble. I know that he keeps a copy of the key to the pantry inside the lining of his coat, and I have seen him more often than not pilfering small quantities of supplies in my mother's absence and hiding them in a box behind the outhouse to take with him when he goes on his weekly furloughs. Because we have equal power over each other, we have a truce.

When the school lets out at four, Hassan Agha is waiting at the bus stop to take me home. Today it is snowing hard and flakes are as big as saucers. Everything is already covered in white. In the falling snow, Hassan Agha looks like a faint silhouette against the wall. His face reminds me of pieces of fluffy clouds, the ones I see in the sky and know they are people of thousands of years ago. Some of them have crowns and long beards and ride horses across the night sky. If you look carefully into the moon, you will see a little girl squatting, with her head on her knees, crying. I keep pointing her out to my stupid brother, who says he can see nothing of the sort.

My mother has an unnatural fear of the full moon and tells me not to stare at the stars, but I do and sometimes see a dragon glide out of the deep blue of the sky and disappear into the Milky Way. When I tell Hassan Agha about it, he screams and pulls the blanket over his head and falls into a fit of loud praying.

There is no sign of the Shemiran bus. Joyfully, I slip and slide on the snow in the middle of the street and kick the trees to shake the snow off their branches. Hassan Agha, shivering furiously, is carrying my satchel and lunch box. His breath condenses faintly in the freezing air. He is wearing my father's old shoes, which are several sizes too big for him, and flakes of snow fall in the gap behind his heel. Because his hands are so small, he is wearing my mother's gloves, except that they are not a matching pair. One is leather and the other fishnet. For New Year's Day, my father orders new suits, socks, shirts, and underwear for the household staff. But Hassan Agha does not wear his new clothes. Instead, he saves them in a suitcase to take them to his village when he goes on leave in the summer. Or he sells them and keeps the money in the stovepipe in his room. I am the only person that knows where he keeps his money. But I swear I never touch it.

I can hear the groan of the approaching bus. Hassan Agha jumps up, but I am not sure if we will board this bus. "If the bus flicks its lights," I tell myself, "we'll get on it. Otherwise we'll wait for the next one, even if Hassan Agha freezes to death and my mother is worried sick by our delay." This is a secret that no one else knows about. It is just between me and Aziz Agha. Even Hassan Agha does not understand why I board some buses and not others. (A bus that does not flick its light is not driven by Aziz Agha.) Hassan Agha yells at me to get on, but I refuse. He has threatened to report me to my mother, but I faintly point to the pantry key in the lining of his coat and he gives up. Before I go to bed at night, instead of the prayer my mother has taught me, I repeat three times, "I will not board any bus not driven by Aziz Agha!" This is a vow between us in effect till Resurrection Day. Of course this vow is unspoken. Because I dare not exchange words with my gigantic friend, who is taller than my father, and his frightful face scares even the policemen.

The oncoming bus flashes its headlights and my heart jumps. When the bus stops, we get on, with Hassan Agha leading the way. Aziz Agha looks at me with his puffy, bloodshot eyes and acknowledges my greeting. His hair is curly and drips with hair oil. Hassan Agha is convinced he gets a perm regularly. He has thick black eyebrows and a bushy mustache that almost covers his mouth. I take the seat directly behind him, and Hassan Agha goes to the back of the bus where there is more warmth and proceeds to fall asleep. There are only a few passengers on the bus, all of them dozing off. It is a long journey from school to our house, especially on snowy days, when some cars that have no chains lose traction in the middle of the road and hold up the traffic. On some days Aziz Agha is more tired than others and yawns massively. His breath, sharper than the smell of the iodine tincture my mother applies to my cuts and bruises, makes my head spin and my belly churn. He looks at me in the mirror and makes faces, blowing up his cheeks, twitching his nose, crossing his eyes. I cover my mouth so that passengers will not hear the sound of my hearty laughter. My friend has the look of a giant, scary enough to frighten small children. His hands and upper chest are covered with tattoos. There is a thick, bluish scar from one ear to the other side of his neck, as if somebody had tried to cut his head off.

My mother never rides the bus. She has her own car and driver because she knows there are monsters like Aziz Agha roaming the world. She is unhappy about my riding the bus to school. But this is my father's direct order and cannot be contravened.

Hassan Agha is fast asleep at the end of the bus. A biting, cold wind blows in from the broken window of the bus, and the passengers are clearly feeling the blast. Aziz Agha takes his jacket off and spreads it over my legs. Its smell assails my nostril, but I am hoping that the gesture has not gone unnoticed by the passengers. With a sense of pride I rub my fingers on the greasy collar of the jacket, and they take on an unfamiliar smell, a smell that is not in our house, nor in my aunts' and uncles' houses. It is not the smell of cats, dogs, and cattle, either. It is a smell that exudes from the corners of an unknown world, of naughty things that should be avoided and things that it is too soon for me to know about.

My mother smells different from anything else. Hers is the smell of perfume and powder, of film stars, fashion magazines, Lalehzar Avenue, and the Municipality Dance Hall. Mother smells of future days, of to-morrow, and all the good things that are in store for me.

But with this jacket on my knees, I am reincarnated. I am someone else, someone who does not have to be clean, polite, studious, and at the top of the class. Someone who does not have to wear a ribbon in her hair, curtsey to strangers on social occasions, and sing her half-learned school songs for them. Someone who does not have to play on the piano her first music lesson, which is not anything more than Do, Re, Mi. Fa,

Sol, La, Ti, for bored and disinterested relatives, and take part and consistently lose in Beautiful-Child contests. With Aziz Agha's jacket on my legs, I become like him, my body covered with tattoos and my mouth full of gold teeth. I feel I am solitary and unescorted, walking the back alleys of the town, or like the daughters of Fatemeh, the laundress, giggling coquettishly and flirtatiously. I feel as if I am riding pillion on the motorcycle of the best-looking boy in the neighborhood, on the way to see the newest Tarzan movie. When we arrive at Abshar Station, Aziz Agha stops the bus. Some passengers get off to drink hot tea in the café, but I stay put. Before he gets off, Aziz Agha produces a little packet from the glove compartment and drops it in my lap. He winks as he eyes me in the mirror. There is a glow of kindness about him, and his face, creased with soft lines, looks like that of a rag doll. My friend is the gentlest giant in the world. I am entranced by the magical, transparent vapor that arises from the strange smell of his breath, his bloodshot eyes, and greasy old jacket. I feel a state of beatitude and an overpowering desire to remain here in statuesque immobility for many millennia to come, without changing, without growing up.

Today, Aziz Agha has given me dried sour cherries. I ignore Hassan Agha, who wants to know what I am doing, and hurriedly count the cherries. The passengers are drinking tea as they stand outside the bus and Aziz Agha takes a swig or two of vodka from his flask. He then goes behind a tree to urinate. I turn my head away and pop the cherries in my mouth in rapid succession. But in my head, I have a vision of him behind the tree and my ears feel hot.

We get back on the road again and wend our way slowly to Vanak Square. Sometimes, the bus slides backward. Other cars lose control and stop in front of us, bringing us to a halt. It is now getting dark and the whiteness of the snow is pervasive. Hassan Agha is rapidly losing heart and keeps calling me from the back of the bus. I know that in a matter of minutes he will start to cry. He is very facile with his tears, and several times a days they flow without any apparent provocation. My mother says that his tears, like the clacking of mother hens, are for no reason at all. My father calls him a pure, unadulterated jackass, which, strangely enough, pleases Hassan Agha. He laughs as he removes the dishes from the table, content that my father is happy with his cooking.

The window next to my seat is broken and the cold wind blows on one side of my face. My neck is stiff and my back feels like a block of ice. Aziz Agha look at me with concern, stops the bus, and stuffs the hole with newspaper and old rags before he resumes his seat behind the wheel. I know his silent language. I know he is concerned and wants me to change my seat. "Get up, you little stubborn girl," his eyes tell me. "You're going to catch your death of cold. Move to the back of the bus. It's warmer there. I am afraid you're going to get sick."

"No way I'm going to move from my special seat," I project as I look at him churlishly.

I am gratified by his concern. It shows the depth of his friendship. I close my eyes and am transported into the fantasy world of bygone ages, when heroes walked on beds of hot coals and defied death by taking on seven-headed dragons to demonstrate their allegiance to their king.

The bus is now completely immobilized and the cold has permeated everything. The right side of my body is numb and my toes tingle furiously. I have no sensation in my shins and my head feels heavy and fluctuating in size. Through the slits in my eyelids, I see shadowy figures moving around in the snow. My nose is dripping and my eyes burn. I have hot flashes followed by violent fits of shivering and chattering of my teeth. I sob uncontrollably. With the soft tips of his fingers, Aziz Agha wipes the tears off my cheeks.

Some of the schoolchildren who know him say that all Aziz Agha's teeth are gold. I don't believe this and I ask my mother about it. She does not know. She does not even know what I am talking about. I can tell she does not like my asking and angrily forbids me to look at or talk to bus drivers and such, or she will have me skinned alive. In her view people with gold teeth are thugs and murderers who will hurt little girls if they get a chance. I can't seem to agree with her. It bothers me to see my mother sometimes say things that are openly spiteful and malicious; for example, when she says that Aunt Azar is fat and ugly. I am also saddened by my mother's ignorance: she does not know the capitals of many countries and is stumped by simple mathematical computations.

Nevertheless, in my view she is the best and prettiest mother in the world, and before I go to sleep at night I feign some kind of ailment so she will sit by my bed. Sometimes I want to confess that I have entertained bad thoughts about her. But she is always in a hurry and has no time for my gibberish. She would punish me severely if she found out that I have eavesdropped when she has been talking to my father.

Aziz Agha is flustered to the extreme by the bogged-down traffic. He tries desperately to untangle the bus and move it forward, but it is no use. It seems like we are lost in a white, trackless desert. From the back of the bus, I can hear Hassan Agha's moans and loud, fear-induced hiccups. I feel queasy and I know it is because of the onslaught of a serious illness. The cherries are bloated in my tummy and I am nauseous. I am holding Aziz Agha's old jacket close around me and feel dizzy. I try to get up but have no sensation in my legs. I open my mouth but cannot make any sound. The snow has covered everything, the bus, the city, and I am frozen in this white space. I have been preserved in this state for years. It is only my eyes that glow like windows of a furnace. Tears roll down my cheeks, and I have a bitter dry taste in my mouth thirsting for water, water, water.

A cool, perfumed hand sweeps across my forehead. Someone whispers a prayer in my ear and blows on my face. Faintly recognizable faces circle my bed, and I identify Aunt Azar's doe eyes under the shining lamp. The smell of Bibi Jan's medicinal tea is in the air. I recognize the soft blanket and clean, crisp sheets of my own bed. My mother is standing there and I feel secure. I go back to sleep, and in my dream Aziz Agha is carrying me on his shoulders as he flies through the air and over the clouds like a flying carpet, taking me to distant, unknown cities. I wish he would open his mouth and let me see his gold teeth. But as always, he smiles with his mouth closed and his lips are sealed like the lid of a treasure chest.

I am gravely ill. Dr. Kosari visits once a week, every Thursday, and finds the whizzing sound of my breathing disturbing. My temperature spikes at night, and he tries a new drug with every visit. But my condition continues to deteriorate. I am thin, sallow, and moribund. I am also losing my hair. I have now a new doctor who coughs harder than I do. He prescribes drugs that aren't available in any pharmacy.

Days and weeks go by with a dizzying speed. Lessons and school are things of the past. Coughing keeps me up all night, and my grandmother stays awake by my bedside to spoonfeed me and entertain me with her stories. Everyday, I look out of the window at the bare branches of the persimmon tree and long for spring. I have visions of the Shemiran bus passing by the school every afternoon at four, with Aziz Agha anxiously looking for me at the bus stop. On the other hand, he may have forgotten me. He may be giving the snacks in the glove compartment to another child. I feel insanely jealous at the thought and fall into a painful fit of coughing. My mother hastily phones the doctor to report the condition, and my father becomes more convinced that I should be taken to Europe for treatment.

I am going to fail school this year and the thought makes me cry. My Aunt Azar tries to console me by insisting that health is more important than anything else. I wish the summer would come sooner and bring a profusion of leaves and fruit to the cherry tree. Our house is even more crowded in the summer. Our family is really a big tribe. I have scores of aunts, uncles, and cousins. My father is generally regarded as the nominal chieftain. In summer time, the entire family dines in our house on Fridays, and my mother keeps half of the guests overnight. We all sleep on the terrace, with the children arranged side-by-side in a row and grown ups scattered under poplars on wooden slats in the mosquito netting. Only my father sleeps by himself in the arboretum, which has a small stream running around it, making lilting sounds through the night. The grandmother sleeps next to the children and keeps an eye on them. She leaves a large glass of iced water next to each bed and a fistful of jasmine petals under each pillow. At bedtime, she takes a head count to make sure every one is present and accounted for.

I simply love the living silence of the summer nights. I can hear the throbbing of ripe fruit and the light breathing of young shoots. Before I drift off, I count the stars and try to find human shapes in the clouds. There is always one that looks like Aziz Agha, calling to me from up there and making funny faces. The boys whisper at each other, and my grandmother strikes their feet with a long switch that she keeps next to her bed. Little Uncle snores mightily, enough to get a response from the stray dogs in the neighboring empty lot. Bibi Jan talks in her sleep and Tooba Khanum scratches herself noisily. Occasionally, one of the children breaks wind and the odor wafts all over the place. My grandmother sits up angrily demanding to know who is responsible. We all pretend to be asleep and not a sound is heard from anybody.

Finally, sleep, accompanied by the buzz of mosquitoes and twinkling of stars, fills every eye. Some nights there is a sprinkling of rain. My grandmother has a large sheet of plastic ready at hand, which she spreads all over us. Under the cover, my cousin and I hug each other and, like ants under the ground, listen to the drops of rain as they hit the thick plastic over our heads.

Since the beginning of my sickness, I have been quarantined in a room. I am scared of everything and I sense the presence of fear everywhere. Sometimes it pokes its head into my room or haunts me in the afternoons when grown-ups are taking their naps. I can see it behind the windowpane or even hiding under my mother's skirt. I swear I saw it in the mirror this morning, sticking out its tongue at me. It is fear that sets off those bouts of coughing.

My mother does not trust the doctors any more, and their prescribed medicines are jettisoned. One of my uncles who is a medical doctor stays overnight on a regular basis. He and my mother alternate in giving my nightly injections. My father is becoming more and more convinced in the genius of European doctors. They cure any disease with one prescription, he says. Aunt Azar eyes me morosely and showers me with kisses as if she'll never see me again. Hassan Agha shows me an old postcard picture of a plump woman with golden hair and in a velvet dress. This is the Queen of Paris, according to him. She is a vicious woman and does not believe in the Holy Koran or the Prophet. He is visibly worried about me and urges my grandmother to say even more prayers for my recovery.

My mother enthusiastically packs multiple suitcases for the projected trip to Europe. But I know fear will be in Paris, too. Now my grandmother is almost incessantly at prayer. Tooba Khanum forces a large cup of liver extract down my throat every evening and has festooned my neck and ankles with all kinds of talismans. There is a heap of small, folded pieces of paper under my pillow.

Still, every day around four in the afternoon, I visualize the Shemiran bus passing by the school and disappearing in a white cloud of dust like a half-forgotten dream.

Still, before I fall asleep at night, I repeat three times the vow: "I will not board any bus not driven by Aziz Agha." I have sworn an oath of loyalty and I will keep faith till Resurrection Day.

I close my eyes firmly and hold my breath as I repeat the incantation. My heart beats resoundingly in my chest, and I am sure Aziz Agha will hear it and make his response known to me somehow.

Departure date has been set for three days from today. My grandmother is sitting by the window busy stringing jasmine buds to make necklaces and wristbands for me. The gloom is pervasive. Even the usually ebullient Tooba Khanum is pensive and teary-eyed.

There is someone at the door. It must be a new doctor or one of the army of visitors and well-wishers who come to see me daily.

Hassan Agha bursts into the room and stands motionless by the door. He looks confused as he glances at my mother. He wants to say something but cannot phrase it. He is hiccupping with nervousness and is making vague gestures to indicate the presence of something or someone outside. My mother, flustered and impatient, follows him into the corridor. "Who is it?" I can hear her shout but not Hassan Agha's response. My mother's voice rises as the sound of an alarm and causes apprehension in all.

My grandmother gets up, closes the window and pulls the blanket to my chin. "The bus driver?" My mother's voice booms in the hall. My heart misses a beat and I sit up in my bed. Hassan Agha's response is plaintive, like the bleating of a sheep about to be slaughtered. My mother's voice echoes in my head: "Who? What? Which bus?"

Poor Hassan Agha is now completely incoherent. I can hear my mother's indignant pronouncements about the gall of a common bus driver presuming to pay her daughter a visit and her command to Hassan

Agha to tell him that if he is seen in the vicinity once again his shins will be broken.

I push off the blanket and jump out of bed. I run in my nightshirt toward the hall. Tooba Khanum tries to restrain me. I push her aside and bite her wrist. My mother, completely taken aback, shouts at me to return to my room. But I ignore her as I throw myself into my father's study at the end of the hall and lock the door behind me. The window looks onto the street. I push the curtain aside and look out. Like a shy little boy, Aziz Agha is standing in the middle of the sidewalk looking very bewildered. He is holding a small packet in his hand. His usually disheveled hair is neatly combed and his shirt buttoned all the way up, perhaps to hide the tattoo on his chest. I open the window and call his name. He looks around and starts walking. I call him again, louder, as I wave at him vigorously. He turns, looks up, and sees me. His face is immediately transformed with the old familiar kindness. Tears stream down my face and I mutter incoherently. He nods at me from where he is standing and a wave of visible happiness rises in his face. He begins to smile, and a strange vision overtakes me as for the first time I see him smiling with parted lips. His open mouth appears like a dark cavern. Somewhere deep inside there is a gold tooth that shines like a magic lamp. Intuitively, I know that all my wishes will be granted by this lamp. I close my eyes and hastily wish that I may be hale and hearty again, that the wracking cough may go away, that fear may leave me forever.

When we arrived in Paris, we checked in at the Vagram. Three days later I was seen by a French physician, who prescribed a long list of drugs. But the process of recovery had started many days before and by then the cough had already gone. No one had any inkling as to my secret magic lamp. My mother, naturally, attributed my improved health to the miracle of European medicine. But I knew what had healed me. Every night, in the darkness of my bedroom I passed my hand over the imaginary magic lamp and intoned my usual prayer.

We stayed in Paris just over six months. When we returned to Tehran, I was matriculated at a new school a block or so from our house and I could walk. But I continued to look for the old Shemiran bus every time I crossed the street.

The years passed rapidly and I grew into a proper miss. The old buses were phased out and, in time, they were replaced by limousines driven by young drivers. However, I remained faithful to my great friend and our secret vow. Whenever I was depressed or had to face a tough situation, there was the sudden flash of the gold tooth across clouds of childhood memories and it always brought me comfort and reassurance.

Another Number 70 bus appears round the corner and slowly moves toward us. In my ear a child's voice says; "I will never board any bus not driven by Aziz Agha."

My daughter goes ahead of me and waves at the driver. Her eyes are brimming with childhood petulance. Perhaps she has a secret of her own that she does not tell me, as I did not tell mine to my mother, or Hassan Agha, or even the poplar trees at the far end of our garden.

My Little Friend

Summer of 1984. Every inch of the French Riviera is carpeted with people. No room to move. I agreed to the trip for the sake of the children, and I regret the decision already. The supposedly blue sea looks dirty and tinged with grey. The air, hot and humid, weighs heavily on my body. I close the book I am reading and look aimlessly over the bodies all around me. My gaze stops on a face distantly familiar. Not very far from me, a woman about my age is stretched out on the sand. A peculiar sense tells me I know her. At the back of my head there is a scrambling of thoughts. In their midst, some memories flash like lightening bugs. I turn away, but I can't shake off the nagging sense. I feel restless and have a compulsive urge to change my place. I call the children. The woman takes off her sunglasses and rummages in her handbag. She lifts her head and looks around—and for a fleeting moment stares at me. It is from her eyes, those big, round, blue eyes, that I recognize her. I feel a tremor down my spine as I did in those childhood days. "Svetlana!" I ejaculate uncontrollably. And with that, an old wound opens up deep down in my bosom. It is Svetlana and yet it is not. Something more voracious than time has ravaged her beauty and freshness. She looks aged and unsightly, depressed and damaged. I see no traces of her long, golden hair, rosy cheeks, white gleaming teeth. How sad, how pitiful, how unbelievable!

Svetlana! I still feel an onset of anxiety at the sound. I try to block the rush of memories, but my heart races and I forget the children and where I am. Countless flickering pictures of Svetlana, as if scrambled by a whirlwind, are scattered in my head, breaking down the flimsy partitions of time, like it was just yesterday, the morning before . . .

I am twelve years old and, by all accounts, the luckiest child in the world. I have my little friend for a playmate, and our friendship is for ever. "From now on, you and I are one," her mellifluous, young voice echoes in my head. "What happens to you will happen to me too. When one of us is gone, the other won't hang on. Friends, friends, till the world ends."

It is in the garden of our family compound in Shemiran that we swear an oath of eternal friendship. We hide behind the poplars and wait till others are gone. We watch Hassan Agha, the cook, tie together by their hind legs the three mice he has caught, douse them with kerosene, and set fire to them. Moments later he returns with two chickens which he deftly slaughters.

By and by, traffic dies down and my friend says, "Are you ready?"

I am. My heart is brimming with an odd mixture of fear and anticipation. I close my eyes and extend my hand. I feel the sharp edge of the razor blade on my skin. I suppress a scream. If I cry, I lose face. I shudder and feel nauseous as warm blood runs down my hand. If I pass out, the bond is annulled, I tell myself. I whisper, "From now on, you and I are one."

Feverishly under my breath, I say the prayer Grandma has taught me to get good grades, hoping it'll also hold back tears. Now it is my friend's turn. With unbelievable courage, she holds up her hand and with one stroke cuts the skin. She does not flinch or squirm. We press the fresh wounds together. Our blood is now mixed. "Friends, friends, till the world ends," we jointly chant.

I have a strange sensation in my body. I am metamorphosed into my little friend. Half of her is in me, and I can distinctly feel the beating of two hearts in my chest. That night I am so excited I can't sleep. "I love my little friend and I'll die without her," I scribble in my composition binder.

For most school children, summer means a hiatus in friendships. But not for me and my friend. We see each other every day and together explore the dark mysteries of the garden. We lie still in the tomato patch and listen to the crickets chirping to high heaven. We catch the frogs that populate the irrigation ditch by the garden wall. They actually croak all night and keep my mother awake. She customarily rewards those who catch them. In a box, we raise silk worms and give their colorful cocoons to other children in exchange for snacks. We cover our lips with petals of red geraniums and dance together, pretending to be grown-ups. Sometimes, we light up a discarded cigarette butt and puff on it in turns, muttering the few words we have learned in English. In the afternoons we range all over the Mahmoudieh Subdivision on our bicycles. By the way, in winter, we had been able to see the Shah skiing with Queen Soraya on the slopes of nearby hills.

Our family estate is in Shemiran and many miles from Feeruzkuhi School. My father leaves for work in his car every morning at seven-thirty sharp. He will not wait for those who are late, not even my mother. And I am always late. My friend waits for me at a nearby intersection to take the bus to school with me. She is often penalized on account of my tardiness. That's why I love her; that's why I'll die for her; that's why I'll do whatever she wants me to.

In class we sit together. Our seats are side-by-side. Everybody knows this, the kids and the teachers. We have been inseparable, like Siamese twins, since first grade. My friend is a tomboy, has short black hair, and despises all those prim little girls in freshly pressed uniforms and white collars. I happen to be one of those when I leave home. But by the time I get to school, I have undone the ribbon in my hair, muffed up my polished shoes, and stained my fingers with ink. Somehow, my friend manages to top the class without any studying. She has no satchel, no books, nor binders that I have seen. In class, she ignores the teacher and surreptitiously reads her favorite books. And yet she aces most quizzes and examinations. I aspire to be like her. I imitate her slavishly in whatever she does. To me, nothing in the world is as important as our friendship. Sometimes I think I love her even more than my mother. In my arithmetic binder, I have written in pig Latin, "I adore my little friend."

Somehow, my friend always has money. She comes and goes by herself, unaccompanied, unchaperoned. If she wished, she could stay with us overnight, without having to get anybody's permission. I don't know where she lives or with whom. I have a vague notion that her mother is divorced and lives in Europe and her father is a notorious gambler. Sometimes he wins a house or property but soon loses everything, and my friend is sent off to stay with strangers, people I don't know and never meet.

Just thinking of the way she lives makes me dizzy. In our household, everything has its niche; there are rules and regulations for everything; nothing is permitted to happen unexpectedly. But my friend comes from a world that is mysterious and forbidden to me, a world that is different from mine. And yet all my prohibitions break down when I am with her. In her company, it is easy to do such things as playing hooky, ripping off the candy store at the street corner, or roaming the street (needless to say, unbeknownst to my mother or any other adult).

Some afternoons, when school lets out, we hide behind the water tanks and wait for everyone to leave the campus. Nobody may stay on campus after hours. But we do. With us, it is a point of honor to break the rules (so says my friend—and I unquestioningly concur). To be alone in those big, empty classroom fills me with a strange exhilaration. It is like venturing into unknown, unchartered territory or experiencing a fever-induced delirium full of garishly bright colors, strange amorphous shapes, and sudden, unforeseeable turn of events. The school after hours changes into something else: corridors seem longer and staircases more tightly spiraled. The place is full of strange shadows and hums with fearsome echoes. The pervasive silence of the building imbues me with thoughts of unspeakable deeds, and I see the furniture change color before my eyes. In the yard, the trees stretch to new heights and, inside, closets emit disturbing odors. We prowl in the halls and do what we wish. Deep down, I fear this freedom. I am aware of the unremitting presence of an invisible eye watching my every move. I feel I must restrain my urges. But my friend pulls me after her and causes my mother's advice and my father's potential wrath to recede to the far corners of my subconscious.

Sometimes we skip a Home Economics or Religious Knowledge class and run down to the city's main drag, where we rush from store to store, occasionally shoplifting dried berries and candy from the confectionery shops. We go past the Setareh movie theater, which almost always shows Russian films. My friend and an elder sister go there often. "This theater belongs to the Communist Party," whispers my friend. I don't know what kind of people communists are. But my brother is in the neo-Nazi party and my cousins are ultra-nationalists, or so I am told. I know no communists in my family. My friend, on the other hand, considers herself the defender of the dispossessed and in that spirit scribbles "Down with the Shah" on the palm of her hand. I shudder at the thought of my mother catching her in the act. She'd have me skinned alive and my friend expelled from school.

The days of summer pass with lightening speed. Like New Year's Eve, the night before the first class day is fraught with excitement. New classes, new school supplies, new lessons. And one more step forward. Soon we'll be thirteen. And fourteen looms ahead. "Fourteen" seems to us the gateway to the world of the grown-ups, a mysterious and scary place. We try not to talk about it but we feel its approach. It makes our hearts beat faster lest it means a parting of the ways.

The sixth form is on the third floor, overlooking the boys' side of the campus. Some girls write unsigned notes and drop them through the window to the other side.

It is the first class of the New Year and we have spelling and dictation. Like always, my friend and I are sitting together. We carve our names on the desk and exchange our pencils, lightheartedly and with glee. Our pockets are already full of flat rocks in preparation for the hopscotch game.

The door opens and there stands the headmistress. We all jump to our feet and stand at attention. We look at her in awe and complete silence. With her is a tall, slender girl, framed by the doorway. She doesn't look like any one of us. She is not even like me or my friend. Her hair is long and blond, and she has big blue eyes. The headmistress calls her to her side. Her name is Svetlana, announces the headmistress. She is Russian and is not as conversant in Persian as the rest of us. So she'll need help from one of us for the rest of the year. But who? The headmistress skims the class in a quick glance and calls my name. Me? "Pick up your satchel and go sit in the back row," she commands, to make room for the newcomer.

I am flabbergasted, dazed. I look at my friend. She is staring at the new girl, baffled and curious. Our place is next to each other. This is the abiding rule of our friendship. Everyone knows that. I am immobilized. I can't move. My friend, perplexed and visibly anxious, looks at the three of us. Slowly I pick up my bag and close its lid. But no, I can't! Why don't these idiots realize that this is my place, next to my friend? We are inseparable. We have sworn an oath of eternal friendship! The headmistress repeats her command, louder this time and with more force. Slowly, I retreat to the back of class and sit next to a girl whose name I don't know and don't care to know, fighting back tears. My friend, too, is upset and angry. She scratches the desk with her pencil and chews on a fingernail. She half rises, as if to protest. She turns and looks at me across the room. By now Svetlana is ensconced in my seat, next to my little friend. Everything has happened so fast. The headmistress mumbles something about my friend helping Svetlana all year. All year, away from my friend? This is unbearable! My seat and hers are now worlds apart, it seems. Between us now there are a thousand barriers, a thousand cities, mountains, seas. For the first time now we have been torn away from each other. I cannot help but notice that Svetlana is talking to her. Perhaps she is telling my friend her last name (a real tongue-twister that I haven't learnt to this day). They seem to have hit it off. It's as if they have known each other for years. Svetlana scratches something on my desk. I am dying to know what. I'd give anything to hear their conversation. The girl next to me pokes me with her elbow to get my attention. She smiles. I take an immediate dislike to her. She looks ugly, stupid, lazy, and I involuntarily squirm. She shows me a notebook plastered with decals of birds. She still looks ugly and insipid, and I pull away from her. I miss my friend and cannot shake off the thought that she is talking to Svetlana. What are they talking about? What? What? What? My head swims as if with fever. The girl next to me stinks. She is a reject and I am embarrassed to be her neighbor. Somehow, I know Svetlana smells good. She probably knows things we can't even dream of. I am pained by jealousy and my stomach is in a knot. Who on earth is she? Where in God's name did she come from or why? I have a premonition of bad things to come. I catch a glimpse of the scar on the back of my hand and sink in the depths of self-pity. Why doesn't my friend object? Why is she tolerating this monstrous stranger sitting next to her? Blood rushes to my head and I jump to my feet bolt upright. The whole class looks at me in bewilderment. The teacher has her head in the book and doesn't see me. "Begin writing," she utters, "new paragraph."

Students get ready to take down the dictation. My friend looks at me and motions me to sit down. She is clearly concerned. I see Svetlana getting ready to write. No! I'm not going to sit down. I am not going to write. My heart is now racing. I am driven by a force that transcends courage. It is insanity perhaps or sheer stupidity. Whatever it is, I have never felt it before. It courses through my body and propels me forward. I leave my seat and start walking in the isle. I have no idea what I am doing. I walk as in a dream. Before I get to where Svetlana is sitting, I hear my name. It is the teacher. Her voice rings in my head. "Return to your seat, you donkey," she yells. I have never been her favorite; she knows I cheat. I don't move, but my knees begin to shake. "Leave the room. Get lost," she hisses.

My friend is now rising from her seat in my defense. The teacher, who likes her and is flustered by the situation, rushes forward, grabs me by my braided hair and drags me to the front of the room. I am now certain that the worst possible punishment is awaiting me. "Jeer at her," she orders the class. But before the class can begin the humiliating ritual, my friend lunges toward me and grabs my hand. The teacher slaps us both—me harder than her—while the jeering is going on. Coolly and maliciously, Svetlana looks on. The teacher screeches threats that if we do not get back to our seats, we will be expelled. But I am satisfied, even happy. My friend and I have scored a victory of sorts and are regarded admiringly by the class as heroes. Back at my seat, I tell myself, "Everything will be as before. Everything."

But Svetlana soon resumes her tête-à-tête with my friend. My feeling toward her has not congealed into hatred. She is not like us. She is well shaped and fair-skinned. I feel her superiority. I am now resigned to the fact that this blue-eyed stranger is here to stay and to ruin the game.

A week has now lapsed since Svetlana took my place. She will not leave my friend alone, even during the recess. Contrary to expectations, her performance in the class is outstanding. She is especially strong in mathematics and wins in all the games we play. But I continue to shun her. Three is always a crowd, I feel. My friend dismisses my apprehension, saying that our friendship is forever. In fact, we upgrade our friendship to a bond of sisterhood, which has its own codes. For example, we must not accept edibles from a third party or play with others. But my friend bends the rules by including Svetlana, pleading sympathy for her isolation. She urges me to be kind to her, too. No, not me! Svetlana is my enemy. She has usurped my place and like a monster has stolen my friend. Besides, she is Russian, probably a communist, patronizing the Setareh movie theater. She enjoys liberties I don't. She could stay overnight wherever and whenever she wants. She lives with a doting aunt and does not have to put up with a mother. In short, she is everything I am not. I cannot compete with her for the affection of my friend because they are so much alike. Some nights I cry myself to sleep and pray vehemently for her death. I start skipping meals and scare my mother. I am having inexplicable bouts of coughing. Through all this, my friend is even kinder to me than before. She brings me snacks, books, and knick-knacks. She has even scrawled my name on the palms of both her hands. At leave-takings, she hugs and kisses me, something she never did before. She even lets me win in hopscotch. But I have a feeling all this is contrived and unspontaneous. It looks like she pities me. The more she placates me, the more I pout and scowl. "That shitty Svetlana is not my friend, but I am supposed to help her with her school work," she tells me every chance she gets. Yet she pokes fun at me by chanting, "Jealous, jealous, hurt and don't tell us."

Tooba Khanum, a member of the household staff, knows witchcraft. Reputedly, she is in cahoots with genies and fairies. I confide in her. There is this vicious, vicious girl who's just come to our school. She's a real hex and has come from behind the mountains. The reason I haven't been getting good grades lately, I tell Tooba Khanum, is that she has cast a spell over me. I ask her to do something so that she'll go back to where she came from and not bother me any more.

Tooba Khanum needs an item of Svetlana's property. I pinch her eraser and bring it to Tooba Khanum, who proceeds to break it up into small pieces. On a scrap of paper, she draws pictures of a frog, a snake, and a woman with horns. Together we trudge to the end of the garden, where she picks some nettles and poison ivy, mixing them with crushed seeds of some flowers. She then wraps them all with the bits of the eraser in a napkin. By now the moon is out and it is full. Holding the napkin under the moonlight, she intones some creepy chants. I am scared and have an urge to flee. Finally, we bury the napkin and its contents and return to the house. I spend a restless night, coughing and shivering till morning. I have nightmares of death, falling headlong into a bottomless pit, and getting lost in a strange town. I have a dream of my friend and Svetlana holding my hands and swinging me round and round. I scream because I don't want to play with any one other than my friend. She is mine, mine, I cry in my sleep. I wake up late, get dressed hurriedly, and rush out without breakfast to catch up with my father for the ride to school. But I am too late and he's gone. Everyone's my enemy, even my own father. Frustrated, I throw down my bag, screaming, and kick the unsuspecting Hassan Agha in the shin. I feel the weight of a slab of granite on my chest causing a pain in my entire body unlike any pain I have known before. I feel feverish and unable to control what I do or say. My mother tries to calm me down by administering her old panacea, milk and honey. But it is no use. I throw myself on the bed, bawling. I don't remember having ever cried like this before. My mother hugs me and strokes my hair. She has no idea what's happened and makes no attempt to find out. She only knows that I hurt, and that's all she needs to know. I hold her hand tight, wishing I could tell her, wishing I were still a child, able to find solace in her embrace. Growing up is so hard; just thinking about it agonizes me.

A math quiz looms in the afternoon. My mother practically forces some food down my throat. My stomach churns with distress. Hassan Agha puts on his shoes ceremoniously and we are on our way.

At the school, I find my friend and Svetlana playing hopscotch. They rush to greet me. Some one suggests we play dodge ball before the bell rings. It so happens that my friend and I excel in this game. First, we must form teams. There are ten of us. My heart beats with expectation. My friend is invariably the team leader and gets the first draw. Before Svetlana came, she always selected me as her first choice. But what now? Will Svetlana end up in the opposing team? Wouldn't that be ideal?

My friend must make a choice now. It looks like this is going to be the most decisive day of my life. Will she choose me or Svetlana? "Today," she says, "we'll select in pairs."

"What?!" every one yells in protest. "Why not?" she counters. "We can select in twos or threes." As usual, she has her way, and she pulls me and Svetlana for her team. I am devastated. I can't play because I'm sick, I lie. She gets visibly upset with me. "Spoil sport," she hisses, with a shrug of her shoulders. Distraught and beside myself with rage, I sit and watch the play. Oh God! So when is Tooba Khanum's damned spell going to work?

The math quiz begins and I am running scared. I'm no good at math and, with my friend ignoring me, I am under a lot of stress. My chest feels like it is about to cave in.

There are three problems on the test. I don't understand the first, so I move to the second one. But I am thinking of Svetlana, Tooba Khanum, and witchcraft. God, do something about this monster from the other end of the world. Make her go back to where she came from.

By now, every one is busy writing. I read the third problem. The stupid girl next to me hopes to copy from my paper, which is still blank. She gives me a nudge. "Six times nine?" she whispers? I shake my head. "Eight times seven?" I don't know. I've known the multiplication table since third grade, but I am drawing a complete blank now. Digits float out of my head and dance in front of my eyes. The girl desperately wants some answers, but I have none. She nervously scratches the table and chews the end of her pencil. Time is running out and I can't concentrate. I am nauseous with anxiety.

Those who finish may leave. The teacher is looking at her watch. My friend and Svetlana finish simultaneously and leave together. She is mad at me and does not even look in my direction. Other kids begin to leave. Some are speedily rewriting. The girl on my other side has unbuttoned her skirt and is copying some answers from the notes she has made on her thigh.

Now the room is almost empty and my page is blank. The teacher pulls the sheet out of my hand and goes to her desk. I am still mumbling some figures, with tears running down my face into my collar. Each teardrop that falls on my dress, desk, and notebook turns into a big zero.

That night I can't sleep. Mother blames it all on malnourishment and vitamin deficiency. She prescribes three spoonfuls of cod liver oil a day, beginning immediately. The echo of my friend's voice reverberates in my head: "From now on, you and I are one. What happens to you will happen to me too."

In the dead of night, I jump out of bed, propelled by a strong desire to die, so that my friend dies with me. There is not a sound audible anywhere in the house. The silence fills me with terror. Barefoot, I walk into the hallway. The winter isn't here yet, but the air is very chilly. As I open the living room door, it squeaks. Everybody is asleep except me. I think of my mother's sorrow at my death, and a lump comes to my throat. I can now hear Tooba Khanum, who sleeps in the living room, snoring. That phony witch! I stifle an urge to kick her fat rump. When I step out in the garden, I am immediately chilled to the bone. I have on only a flimsy nightgown. Trees, tall and black, with branches twisted and long like fingers of wizards, seem to frown on me. They sway in the gentle breeze, whispering their disapproval of me in one another's ears. I stand by the side of the pool and watch the pale reflection of the moon in the water. The mermaid statues glare at me from across the pool. They all seem to know why I want to die. But after all, this is our only game in which Svetlana has no role. She will croak with jealousy. I touch the scar on the back of my hand, and a sweet voice sings in my ear: "What happens to you, will happen to me too." How appropriate! Damned Svetlana! This is my game, our game.

I break a twig from a climbing rose bush and press its sticker into the scar of the old wound in my flesh. A thin flow of blood streaks over my hand. It is her blood. My teeth begin to chatter, and an icy sensation runs through my bones, my head, my lungs, my whole body. I close my eyes and count to a hundred. A patrolman's whistle sounds in the distance, and I feel the neighbor's cat rubbing herself against my bare legs. A light comes on in an upstairs window. Some one is awake, probably my father. I am numb with cold and cannot feel my feet. Am I dead? The thought frightens me, and I start running toward the house. The hall door slams with a bang, startling Tooba Khanum who bellows, "Who's it?" Back in my bed, I slip under the covers and pull them over my head. I know that I am now due for a major illness.

The routine begins: visits from Dr. Kosari, drugs, injections, and Mother's anxiety attacks. I have pneumonia and bouts of coughing explosive enough to scare everyone.

Lo and behold, I have a visit from my friend. First, I cover my face with the bed sheet and turn to the wall to indicate my displeasure. But she is not fazed and comes a second time and every other day. She brings schoolwork to catch me up but never mentions a word about Svetlana. Slowly, she begins to look like her old self. My resistance breaks down, and we begin to talk and laugh as in the old days. Sometimes I am tempted to ask about Svetlana but I never do, afraid to raise her specter in our revitalized relationship. I know she is still lurking in the background; other school friends mention her occasionally. But it looks like she has found other company and has left me and my friend alone. I am happy, beatific in fact, and I recover fast. I eat and sleep regularly and can't wait to return to school.

Back at school, I find everything as before. I write the best composition in class and get the best grade. I feel victorious and regain my self-confidence.

The winter is now here and so is my thirteenth birthday. Customarily, I celebrate my birthdays only with my friend, one of the conditions of our bond of eternal friendship.

Svetlana continues to occupy my seat. But I don't care any more. She even offers to vacate it, but with a shrug I say no, thanks. I am now secure in my friend's loyalty and unafraid of this golden-haired enchantress. But I still don't like the tripartite games, which mean sharing my friend with others. She on the other hand says one can be friends with three or ten people. But I don't believe she is quite sincere. This is a ruse to have me and Svetlana both. I know that if Father as much as looked at another woman, Mother would gouge out his eyes. Or if my physician uncle took a mistress, his wife would die on the spot.

For my birthday, Hassan Agha has promised a special dinner and my mother a special dessert. The first snow of the year falls on that day. Everybody is out on the street, snow shovelers yelling, cars skidding, traffic getting tangled up at every intersection. There is a happy bustle all over town, as if the whole world is celebrating my birthday.

In class, I feel drugged and pleasantly drowsy. In my head, numbers look like birthday-cake candles. I count the minutes in anticipation for the end of the school day. Everything is going my way, and I am embarrassingly happy. I will be thirteen tomorrow, just a step away from fourteen. "Fourteen" has a strange chime in my head. It makes my head spin and my ears ring. I repeat the word and arch my back in delight. I imagine myself in love, kissing a faceless boy over and over again. The arrangement is for me and my friend to go home after school and stay overnight. Only the two of us, no Svetlana. At the end of the last period, the teacher takes the roll. When she calls my name, I yell "present" so loud that it makes everyone laugh. At the bell, I jump and throw my bag up in the air. Svetlana, looking pouty and grim, is talking to my friend. She is upset because my friend has chosen me over her. The thought fills me with rapture. "Jealous, jealous, hurt and don't tell us," I murmur.

I dash outside and playfully skid on the snow. Hassan Agha is waiting at the gate to take us home. My friend is looking around, distracted. She is fumbling in her pockets. "Hurry, let's go," I urge her. She does not answer me. She seems discomfited and distant. There is a mystifying look in her eyes. She rubs her cheek, says she has a toothache. I notice Svetlana, in a red scarf and black boots, sauntering out of the school gate, not even looking in our direction. She looks ravishingly elegant. Once again, I feel a twinge of inferiority. I can never compete with her. Once again, I wish her gone, out of the way. My friend follows her with her eyes, which reflect a certain obstinacy, till she disappears round the corner. My friend groans with pain. I have an urge to hug her and kiss her cheeks and her little white hands. I feel for her pain so much that my own teeth seem to ache. I am strangely gratified. We are one. What happens to her happens to me.

No sign of the Shemiran bus yet. My friend says she must call her father and let him know about our plans. This is the first time she has mentioned him, or the need to inform him of her whereabouts. "You go ahead," she exhorts me. "I'll join you later."

I insist that we go together. She seems irritable and fidgety. She groans and rubs her cheek as if to alleviate the pain.

"I've got to see the dentist," she says. "It's a couple of blocks from here. You just go ahead. I'll come by myself."

I almost refuse but, afraid to annoy her, I comply. An icy chill runs through me. My friend wheels around and breaks into a run, disappearing into a narrow street a block away. All my plans have unraveled. Hassan Agha is grumbling bitterly, with snow accumulating on his head. "Let's get going, you brat!" he yells.

But I am thinking of my friend. I should have gone with her. What if she has to have an extraction? What if she is overwhelmed with pain? I should be there to soothe and comfort her. "Wait here," I tell Hassan Agha. "I'll be right back."

Before he has a chance to object, I take off. I can hear him shouting after me that he's had it with me and he won't wait, that he'll in fact go back to his old village this very night, that he'll tell my mother about it. But I hurtle down the street where my friend had gone and find it is a cul-de-sac. Snow has already covered her tracks. To my right there is an empty lot and a house under construction. A short, cinder-block wall runs to the end of the street. I am freezing and try to suppress the onset of coughing. My ungloved fingers are numb. I look for anything that suggests a dentist's office. I find none. All I can hear is the silent fall of snow, a muffled, sleepy murmur. The steady, regular decent of snow-flakes creates a levitating visual effect, as if houses, trees, even I, are float-ing upward. The sensation makes me feel weightless and detached from my surroundings. I am transported to a fantastic world of eternal white-ness.

My friend has vanished, swallowed up by the snow. I start missing Hassan Agha's reassuring presence. The kind and simple Hassan Agha. From a lighted window on an upper floor of a house, a woman's head in flowered scarf juts out. In a language that sounds foreign to me she yells something to the people presumably in the yard. This puts me in mind of Svetlana, and I shudder violently. I am scared and want to go back, but something propels me further down the street. There is a shooting pain in my gums, reminding me of my friend's toothache and my plans to renew our blood oath on my thirteenth birthday! A blood oath banishing Svetlana from between us, for now and ever.

The houses in this street have front yards with wrought iron fences. In the last one, I espy a snowman with large pieces of coals for eyes and a green pencil stuck in his mouth for a cigarette. He wears an incongruent red-flowered scarf on his head. Through the fence, he is staring directly at me. He looks cold and pitiful, with one cheek swollen, as if with an abscessed tooth.

From behind the hedges in the yard, I hear the muffled sounds of children at play, but I cannot see them. A snowball comes flying from somewhere and hits the snowman in the head, nearly knocking off his scarf. I can see through the fence that the scarf is the one Svetlana was wearing this morning. I am sure of it. Snow gets in my eyes and into the back of my neck. I have a strong desire to run, but I am transfixed and cannot move. More than ever I long for Hassan Agha. I can now see two children emerging from behind the hedges and cavorting in the snow near the snowman. The sound of their voices echoes against the walls and down the street. The one facing me is Svetlana. She doesn't see me, though. Her cheeks are flushed, and her golden hair bobs on her shoulders. She is so doll-like it scares me. To me, she is an omnipotent sorceress, and if she notices me she'll skin me alive. Next to her is my friend, with a snowball in each hand. She hurls one at Svetlana and laughs. Svetlana chases her playfully. Their vitality and happiness seem unbounded.

That damned Tooba Khanum and her phony witchcraft!

Reluctantly, my eyes follow my friend, my cheating, lying, disloyal friend. I feel betrayed. This is the first and the biggest fraud ever perpetrated on me.

My fingers are frozen around the fence rods, and tears run down my face. Somewhere in my body—not in my teeth or head or bosom but in my thoughts, my words, and way beyond my heart—there is an agonizing pain, an unfamiliar pain. It is the kind of pain my mother and Auntie Azar sometimes talk about, and it makes them cry.

"Be careful," Tooba Khanum had warned me. "The thirteenth year is ill-omened. Make sure you pray every night."

"You must go to America and be educated," my father decrees. "You must make money and be somebody."

My mother talks of the future, love, marriage, and of feminine mysteries.

I have now broken up with my friend. I haven't told her in so many words, but she knows. Sometimes I catch her looking at me, and somewhere beyond that look is an unspoken word. Perhaps she wants to remind me of our blood oath. But I can't trust her anymore. My heart is clammed up, and I feel hard as a rock.

The year at Feeruzkuhi School comes to an end, and I am sent to a prestigious secondary school in the city. I initiate new friendships, all shallow and transitory. I have love affairs repeatedly and repeatedly cry on their account. But they are all forgotten. All those heart-rending wounds heal without a scar, and time polishes all scratches off my soul. The only thing that remains is the little scar on the back of my hand and the dull pain of a childhood memory associated with it.

Here again is Svetlana, after all these years! She looks like a homing pigeon that has lost its way. She is disoriented, ruffled, and exhausted. I see that Tooba Khanum's spell has worked after all. Svetlana's eyes, still blue and large, are vacant and expressionless. The onslaught of time and countless experiences bitter and sweet have clearly wiped out the memory of that year at Feeruzkuhi School and my little friend.

From the edge of the water, where he is playing with other children, my son calls to me. I hear him and release my bated breath. A huge weight is lifted off me, the weight of an old, bitter, hurtful jealousy. Perhaps I should have played the threesome games. I sink to my knees next to my children. Another being writhes within me and creeps under my skin.

A voice rings deep down in my ears: "Friends, friends, till the world ends."

Grandma's House

At noon on Thursdays, the school closes,[1] not to open again until the morning of Saturday, that shitty day! That's why Thursdays are different from any other day of the week; they are silvery and bright, smelling of good things and promising happy moments. They are cuddly, soft, and soporific, like cozying up to Grandma or leaning back against Mother's ample bosom.

Each day of the week has its own shape, color, and smell: Saturday is ugly, bitter, and obnoxious like Tooba Khanum's old-maid daughter—lanky, beady-eyed, and ill-natured. Sunday is dumb and simple-minded. It drifts aimlessly, getting bumped around by other days of the week. Monday looks like His Grace Heshmat-ol-Mamalek,[2] elegant and dignified, clad in formal grey attire complete with a cane. Tuesday is diffident and serene, giving off a greenish-yellow luminescence. Wednesday is crazy. It is plump and garrulous and smells of lintel rice, deliciously prepared by Hassan Agha, the cook. Thursday is heavenly. Friday has two distinct parts. Until noon, it is lively and energetic; like my father, it is vigorous, athletic, and entrepreneurial. Toward the evening, it becomes increasingly heavy-hearted and morose, beset by vague anxieties and baseless fears. With it come a guilty conscience and a bloated feeling caused by overeating at lunch (stuffed to the gills with meat and rice). And having to do those damned homework assignments to the strains of dolorous music from the radio doesn't help either. That's when I long for Mother to come back from visiting her friends. There is a tinge of dark brown on everything, including the sky, the trees, and the air, on late Friday afternoons.

Traditionally, the whole family has lunch at Grandma's on Thursdays. Hassan Agha is supposed to pick me up at school. He is often late and we quarrel. In a foul mood, he tries to keep up with me as he utters obscenities, cursing himself and all the spoiled brats like me. In his mutterings, he accuses Mother of being responsible for every misfortune befallen him and his entire clan. He vows to give notice the next day and issues many other threats, all of which I have heard a thousand times before and have learned to ignore.

Grandma's house is at the end of a wide street just past Heshmatdowleh intersection. It is a fair distance from my school, but on Thursdays it does not seem more than a few steps. I am so high on the prospect of the weekend that I feel no hunger and fatigue. As I wend my way toward Grandma's house, every alley and street I pass, every ditch (over which I make a point of jumping several times), every policeman directing traffic, every passerby, every automobile, every bus stuffed with passengers, every dilapidated horse carriage, every smell and noise in the public thoroughfare simply punctuates my approach to Grandma's house. No sooner have I seen that heavy oaken door than I lunge for the bell. My entire body dilates with the joy of arrival and only then I realize how tired and hungry I am. I drop my satchel and lean against the wall and slowly slide to the floor. I can just sit there for hours and luxuriate in that blissful state.

Grandma's house is a curious place. A part of it is bright, happy, and familiar, the other dark, sad, and mysterious. At the end of the hallway a big old clock hangs on the wall, and its ticking can be heard in every room in the house.

"This clock," says my mother, " is a hundred-and-fifty years old and will be here after we're all gone." I detest this old tenacious clock! I don't understand what "after we're all gone" means. But I know that it irritates me.

The second floor is off-limits to us children. Past the seventh step on the staircase, lies another world, a world of obscure events, secret sorrows, soft whispers and sobs. One of my mother's brothers—which one, I don't know—lives upstairs. We know that this unseen uncle is sick. If we were asked, we would readily say that this uncle has had it (and suffer the slap in the face for our unseemly callousness). I don't remember having seen this uncle but I always hear the echo of his cough. He is supposedly a painter, and two of his paintings hang in the parlor.

It is always my mother who carries trays of food and medicine upstairs. Her eyes are often red when she comes back. If you asked her why she'd been crying, she'd deny it and say she's got a cold or a mosquito's got in her eye. Grown-ups insist on protecting us children from the unpleasantnesses of the world. But we have Hassan Agha, who eavesdrops behind closed doors. We also have Tooba Khanum, who spies through keyholes. Because she knows witchcraft, she divines every happening and hears every sound. At night, when she is alone with us, she tells us everything.

What Mother does not understand is that we children are not really affected by an uncle's illness or someone else's death. On the contrary, we secretly look forward to such events. For one thing, Grandma makes those ceremonial flour patties we love so much. Also, when in distress, grown-ups are more lenient and accommodating. Why, I don't know and it doesn't matter. The fact is that in those situations they become less demanding and querulous and show more concern if we complain of any aches and pains.

Like her house, Grandma's garden has two parts, good and bad. The bad part is the garage and the pump house, which are always locked up. Tooba Khanum swears she has seen several genies with cleft hooves playing with some cute-looking fairies in the pump house. My brother, enraged by disbelief, pulls Tooba Khanum's hair and tries to trip her up. During the day, I am brave, sensible, and fearless when I pass by the pump house. But at night, I hear haunting sounds emanating from there, and strange shadows ply the trees nearby. My body freezes in a vague and nameless fear. I draw as near as possible to Grandma and avert my eyes from the dark corners of the garden.

In the middle of the courtyard, there is a reflecting pool with an inverted fountain in its center. The fountainhead is of the revolving kind and sprays the area surrounding the pool. Flowerbeds are overgrown with weeds and moribund squash and tomato vines. Only the persimmon tree is in good health and is seasonally prolific. Any unthinking child daring to touch its fruit will be dealt with severely. A few pots of geraniums adorn the border of the pool. At the far end of the courtyard, beds equipped with mosquito netting and clean, flowered sheets are set up for sleeping outdoors during the summer months. At the foot of each bed are thriving, potted jasmine bushes whose fragrance soothes our nostrils even as we sleep. This sleeping facility is reserved for my mother or grandchildren when they stay overnight. My brother and I—and occasionally Dariush, my youngest uncle's son—are the favorites. Auntie Azar's wild brood often misbehaves. So they get their ears boxed and are sent back home forthwith with one of the servants.

Tooba Khanum, Khaleh Khanum, Gohartaj Khanum and Bibi Jan,[3] the elder women in the family, always sleep indoors on the floor of the big living room. All night they put out a cacophony of sneezing and coughing. Or they sit up to massage their swollen, achy feet or frequent the bathroom. Even when they are sleeping, they emit noises of old age: they groan, fart, or heave heavy sighs. To me, though, Gohartaj Khanum is different from others. I find her lovely, always smelling of candy and rose-water. She has blue eyes, silver hair, and ruddy cheeks. She is birdlike and reminds me of the canary that I have heard singing in the trees.

There is a big room over the pump house. Its doors and windows are always shut tight and its curtains drawn. Its exterior is covered with thick ivy. To us it looks like the dwelling of a witch, a witch who devours children. Yet another uncle lives in this ivy-covered room. It is common knowledge that this uncle is an opium addict and, for a hobby, raises pigeons. But he hates children—and everybody else for that matter. Evidently, he once kicked Tooba Khanum and once caught Auntie Azar's children in his room and nearly twisted off their noses and ears! With me and my brother, however, he is more tolerant; probably because he is intimidated by my father.

According to Tooba Khanum, this uncle was at one time very handsome and comely, with big brown eyes and pearly white teeth. But sorrow and remorse have taken their heavy toll—sorrow, remorse *and* love. As he appears now, he has small puffy eyes, rotten teeth, and a sallow complexion. How is it possible to change this much? He has shrunk and decayed beyond belief.

"Wait," warns Tooba Khanum. "Your turn will come too. You'll look in the mirror and scare yourself. Do you think this is how I always looked?

Or Bibi Jan? Life takes you and twists you out of shape. Before you know it you'll be a doubled-up old hag."

Tooba Khanum is mean and a liar. I just don't want to believe a word of what she says. Obviously, she wants to scare me. In my reckoning, beautiful people like my mother stay beautiful forever. It is only those mean fibbers that get old and turn ugly, blind, and bald. This uncle must always have looked like he does now. Tooba Khanum is just ignorant and doesn't know what she is talking about.

Some days this uncle ventures out of his room for fresh air. He squints in the brightness of day as he stands near a flowerbed, muttering unintelligibly. He has two dozen pigeons and spends most of his time with them. Some evenings, he climbs on the roof and watches them as they fly in a circle around the house. Clearly he likes one of them more than others. It is a white one with a golden-reddish ring around its neck. He has named it Maryam, after his ex-wife. And seems to have animated, passionate conversations with it. He carries it in his pocket and sometimes in the fold of his shirt next to his skin. My brother is convinced that these pigeons are addicted to opium too. He has seen them in his room gathered around the smoking paraphernalia, cooing, with the favorite actually perched on his lap.

My mother's injunction is that we must not under any circumstances go near his room or distract him in any way. He is doing research, according to Mother, for a very important book. Likely story! We know all about him, courtesy of Tooba Khanum. He is the way he is because of his wife, or rather, because of his compulsive, irrational love and jealousy for her. He would not let her out of the house. He would keep doors, windows, and curtains closed so she could not catch a glimpse of anyone else. He could not bear the thought of his wife thinking or even dreaming of anyone she might have known before the marriage. Sometimes, he would wake her up in the middle of the night. "Whom were you dreaming of?" he would yell at her belligerently. "Why were you smiling in your sleep?" Why? Why? Why? And so it went on and on, these scarring, hurtful altercations.

Maryam was allowed to leave the house only for her periodic visits to the public bathhouse two blocks away. Even then, she would be followed closely by my uncle who would wait in the lobby to accompany her back to the house. All the while under the guise of reading the paper, he would monitor the traffic in and out of the bathhouse. Then, he would escort her back home and to the usual routine. Then, on one of those visits to the bathhouse, on the last Thursday before New Year's Day, Maryam took longer than usual. Two, three hours and no sign of Maryam. My uncle, impatient and chain-smoking, started getting worried. He paced up and down the lobby and checked his watch every few seconds. What'd happened? Had she passed out? Had she drowned? Eventually, he lost control and kicked down the door to the bath stall only to find it empty! He could not believe he had been duped! (I love this part of the story, especially as Tooba Khanum narrates it. She makes it sound as if she had been there and seen everything with her own eyes!)

There were all kinds of speculations on Maryam's flight. Maybe she had fed him some magic potion to impair his judgment, or had used some witchcraft to become invisible, or had simply disguised herself in an outfit borrowed from Khadija the masseuse. Invariably, I get excited and cheer for Maryam's freedom. Hassan Agha, on the other hand, gets jittery at the mention of magic and witchcraft. He jumps up, says a prayer for his protection, repeatedly muttering "What a lesson! What a lesson!" Actually, he always utters this irrelevant sentence under any circumstances. From this point on, Tooba Khanum becomes even more animated and goes through the rest of the story as she simultaneously downs two or three cups of tea, smokes her water pipe, performs her evening prayer ritual, and thrusts a bowl of pumpkin seeds under our noses. In great detail, she tells how my uncle like a maniac broke into the women's part of the bathhouse and chased the women, pulling off their head covers. He then ran into the street, banging on doors and stopping cars and buses looking for Maryam. In the process, he got into fights with people and was beaten to a pulp before he eventually gave up and returned home.

That night he started running a very high temperature, which persisted on and off for forty days, during which he would hardly eat anything or recognize anyone. He would babble deliriously, just calling his wife's name. All treatment and medication proved ineffectual, even Tooba

Khanum's magical brew. They took him to the seaside, to a sanitarium, and to an asylum for therapy, all to no avail. He kept roaming the house from room to room whimpering a like a disconsolate child or a senile old woman on the verge of death. Once, my father lost his composure and slapped him hard across the face. Surprisingly, this calmed down my uncle, who sat in a corner for several hours in a daze. But then he suddenly jumped up, grabbed a kitchen knife, and started stabbing himself in his chest and belly. For better or worse, the knife had a broken tip and was so dull it wouldn't cut butter, let alone human flesh.

My uncle's malady stumped everyone, until my worldly-wise grandfather thought of a remedy. He ordered the room above the pump house to be cleaned and refurbished. He then took my uncle into that room with a large supply of opium and the wherewithal for smoking it. They stayed there for a whole month, and when they emerged, my uncle was a firm and full-fledged opium addict. Since then he has been quite calm and docile.

I have faint recollections of my kindly grandfather and his brand of wisdom. His facial features, like a faded photograph, are vaguely registered in my head. I remember his light brown hair and mustache. He was a pharmacist, and I loved to play in his shop. I could hide under his desk or in a dark corner and play with the multitude of empty medicine boxes. In my childish ways, I thought of the pink boxes as girls and of the white ones as boys. Usually, girls chased boys. Sometimes they got into a fight and tore one another up. Or they fell in love and got married. The most beautiful box represented my mother. Occasionally, I misplaced it or imagined that it had died. This always made me cry. But when it reappeared, I would beat up on it and try to tear it up to pieces.

In a glass jar on top of the cabinets, there used to be a fetus submerged in a fluid. It had deformed limbs and its head was abnormally large. "Do you see that?" my mother would say. "You looked like that when you were in my tummy." The fetus was perpetually asleep. It didn't grow or change shape. It made me wish I did not grow up either. I am afraid of growing up and looking different from the way I look now.

Some nights I think wistfully of Tooba Khanum's account of my uncle's affair. I picture his withered complexion and elongated nose. This brings tears to my eyes and makes me fearful that my father might some day look like him. I get a bad feeling; something worse than a malady or pain courses through me. If I am by myself, I let out a scream. My mother is flustered by my grim moods, and on two occasions she has confined me to my room. Only Hassan Agha has an intuitive sense that something dark and foreboding troubles me. "It is all the fault of these genies," he opines. "They make you cowardly and vicious. They are behind every trouble in the world."

Hassan Agha's world is populated by a myriad of spectral presences— some good, some bad. Some of the malignant ones get into your head and make you lie and cheat, or malinger just to get out of going to school. They are the ones that cause high prices in staple foods, or make you filch a tooman[4] or two from your father's pocket. It has happened on some occasions that my mother has experienced a sudden onset of toothache, making it necessary for her to pay an emergency visit to Dr. Kosari's office. It is the demon in my head hinting that my mother is lying, that she just wants to get out of the house to go to a movie or visit some friends. Sometimes, when I hear my father yelling on the phone or quarreling with my mother or with Hassan Agha, the demon in my head tells me that my father is malicious and selfish.

"Those who do not respect their parent and harbor doubts of their integrity," intones the teacher in the religious knowledge class, "are doomed to burn in the fires of hell." I have no doubt that the demon in me wants me to burn in hell. He plants suspicions in my head. "Look," he insinuates, "they love your brother more than you. You are a foundling. They are lying to you. You see how they lavish their attention on him, how they praise him? They have got him new shoes and hats. Nobody loves you." I hold my ears and yell, "Get lost you filthy stupid demon!" I shake my head violently to dislodge him from my thoughts.

"Demons are scared of fairies," pontificates Hassan Agha. "Fairies are friends to good children. If you want their favor," he tells me, "say your prayers regularly."

I have discovered one thing: when I am happy, the demons stay away from me, as if something scares them. It seems they thrive in sadness and in the minds and hearts of cowards. These days, however, it seems fairies have the upper hand in my head. I have not entertained any bad thoughts for days and am convinced of my mother's love for me. There is much cause to be jolly. For one thing, next Saturday there is no school because of a national holiday. For another, one of my ugly cousins is being married at the end of the week, and the wedding is at my Grandma's house. She is almost as ugly as Saturdays. Everyone is preoccupied with this rather unexpected event: what gift to buy, what to wear, whom to invite, whom not to invite. Somehow, the list of "don'ts" is longer than that of "do's."

The main concern of course is getting outfitted for the occasion. My mother has her clothes made by Madame Ana. According to my mother, she is *couturiere* to the Queen and has studied fashion design in Paris. My father scoffs at my mother's remarks and asserts that all these beggarly Armenians make such claims. Madame Ana's "salon" is at the end of street in an Armenian neighborhood on the third floor of a dilapidated building. It consist of two dingy rooms that always smell of industrial-strength toilet-bowl cleaners. The Madame has four cats— the most miserable-looking, scrawny, diseased cats in the world. One limps around with a deformed leg; another suffers from mange, with scabs covering its head and tail; another appears to be blind. Everywhere there are small plates of cat food laden with boiled chicken heads and leftover macaroni. In one of the rooms, there are a few wooden mannequins, each sporting a ladies' straw hat decorated with ribbons and tassels. The Madame says she has designed and made them for Princess Ashraf.[5] The next room is the beauty parlor where Madame Ana displays her skin care products and cosmetics. My mother is a regular customer. Madame Ana's ointments smell alternately of garlic and body odor, as does she herself.

My dress, however, is to be bought from Lalehzar Avenue,[6] from a ready-made store on which we all converge: my mother, Auntie Azar, my junior uncle's wife, and I, a few days before the wedding. My junior uncle's wife is a knitting enthusiast and knits with incredible speed. I have never seen her without her knitting needles and yarn. She can knit a cardigan and a bonnet in a day. She knits at home when she walks, talks, and works. She knits when she is on the street or at a party. She knits even in her sleep. She knits clothes for herself, her children, and her husband. All bedspreads, tablecloths, towels, and even the flower arrangements in her house are knitted. She is pregnant and I am convinced that the baby is also knitted of wool and yarn. If it comes out less than perfect or disfigured, it can be undone and knitted again in the desired fashion

We take the bus to Lalehzar Avenue. My mother and aunts have to enter the crowded bus sideways because they are wearing dresses with such wide shoulder pads. They can hardly sit next to one another on the seat. My junior uncle's wife ends up standing up in the aisle. Even then she does not stop knitting. The needles poke other people causing general complaint. At an intersection near Istanbul Avenue, the bus comes to a screeching halt to avoid hitting a startled carriage horse, tumbling the passengers in a chaotic mess. Children scream and I see Auntie Azar clobbering with her fists a plump man sitting next to her, evidently because in the confusion he has fondled her thighs and arms. At this point, we get off and walk the rest of the way. Istanbul Avenue is throbbing with hordes of people. The Azerbaijani citrus vendors advertise their produce noisily. Throngs of hawkers push their wares, and beggars, some of them blind and some with open sores on their faces and heads, persistently accost the shoppers—and my mother, who cusses at them vociferously and to no avail. Worst of all are the loutish loiterers, who pinch the women and hurl salacious insults at them. Auntie Azar takes all this in her stride and appears mildly amused. Only, occasionally, she slings her handbag at a lout in self-defense. My mother, on the other hand, scowls and wards off unwanted attention with threatening glances. The junior uncle's wife carries a hatpin and sticks the molesters with it.

Auntie Azar blushes at suggestive remarks, as if she rather enjoys them. Tooba Khanum has told us a lot about her. She supposedly has a roaming eye and has monthly affairs. Her husband is reputedly an embezzler—and not a nickel-and-dime one either. He is director general of a major government agency with car and driver privileges. He drops hints that he is associated with the Shah. But, in reality, he has only received a couple of invitations to official functions at the court, when he has had dinner with the Queen Mother. He claims that she has a crush on him and gives him money and gifts on a regular basis. This, of course, is a lie, and my father knows all about him. In his news magazine, my father has on several occasions exposed his corrupt practices.

Personally, I just love Istanbul Avenue. The odor of fish and aroma of coffee and roasted nuts and seeds blend in my nostrils, making me feel steeped in languor and drowsiness. I imagine myself a grown-up woman and the object of desire of all the men around me. I fantasize that I have an interminable supply of money, that I am able to buy all the fruit loops and cream puffs my heart desires, that I can go to see "Bathing Beauties" a hundred times.

At the far end of the street, we run into my two youngest uncles. They are both dressed to the nines. They look like film stars, with white shoes and socks and black fedoras. Very elegant. Very handsome. They barely acknowledge us, just tipping their hats to us and walking by.

There is a haberdashery at the top of Mehran Lane. It sells everything from bridal headgear to silk stockings and foreign-made ladies' underwear. The chador-clad women are its most aggressive shoppers. They try brassieres for size by holding them against their chests. For some reason, this embarrasses me deeply. Auntie Azar, a little on the plump side, is looking for high-quality corsets. The sales clerk, elderly and bald, reaches around Auntie Azar's girth with the tape measure to get her size. In the process, he makes some kind of a move that makes her give a little scream and a giggle. "Filthy old man," mutters my mother. The clerk ignores her and gives me a pat on the head and a piece of hard candy.

The next stop is the Pirayesh clothing store. It occupies a two-story building and is the largest such establishment in Tehran. The sales clerk looks clean-cut and well-dressed in coat and tie. In the window, there is a life-like mannequin of a woman in evening dress with a plunging neckline. Some older men, about my father's age, and a few young lads are standing outside the window ogling at the mannequin. Oddly, the scene makes my heart race. Stealthily, I look at the mannequin's breasts, and I feel a churning in my bowels.

We backtrack to Istanbul Avenue to buy my outfit at the Nonahalan, a children's dress shop. I really don't like what they get me. The skirt is too long, and there is a silly velvet cowl hanging from the shoulders. The Bata Shoe Store has recently opened and is still attracting large crowds gaping at latest fashions in footwear. Here, we encounter my two young uncles again, who tip their hats as they pass us by. It seems that is all they do, just walk up and down the street a hundred times a day.

By the time we get back, Grandma's house is a beehive of domestic activity: washing, scrubbing, cooking, baking. Everyone is kind and courteous. The place is redolent with the delicious aroma of food, reminding me of Thursday afternoons. A sense of well-being, warmth, and simplicity permeates the atmosphere.

Hassan Agha, in my reckoning the best and most famous cook in the world, is in charge of catering. He is dressed in new clothes and looks like a million. I climb all over him and give him enthusiastic hugs as he mildly protests. My mother appears perturbed by my show of affection for Hassan Agha. She scowls and her facial expression indicates that she considers my behavior forward and provocative. Wordlessly, she tells me that at the threshold of puberty I must watch out for the way I act around people. The thought sickens me. It seems that adulthood means hypocrisy, inhibition, and loss of spontaneity. To be a lady means to be insincere. To be a good girl is to be deceitful.

According to Tooba Khanum, being a woman is worse than being a dog. "Wait until you grow up," she tells me. "Then you'll see what I mean." That's why I sometimes wish I were a boy. I wear pants and act tomboyish, knowing all the while that there is a big difference between me and boys. Soon, I will have to wear skirts and tie ribbons in my hair. I will have to accept it as facts of life if my brother pulls my hair, kicks me, or takes away my candy.

In the yard, pansies adorn the flowerbeds. Only nineteen days are left until New Year's Day. The fountain is squirting water all around the pool. The air smells of wet earth and flowering jasmine. This tells me that New Year's holiday and summer vacations cannot be far away.[7]

I am startled as I catch a glimpse of my uncle staring at me from behind his window over the pump house. He steps outside, still in his striped pajamas and house slippers. Somehow, he reminds me of a half-eaten, long abandoned plate of food, congealed and desiccated.

Unaccountably, I pity him. I don't understand his kind of being in love—to act like an idiot and then run high fever! My father on the other hand is always stable. He does not yell or indulge in bouts of jealousy. He does not imprison my mother in her room. No one has ever fallen in love like my uncle and suffered as much. What if somebody falls in love with me like that? Confines me to my room and does not let me ride my bike or go shopping in Istanbul Avenue. What if he forces me to do his bidding, or takes away my candy and edibles? Perhaps I could fall in love in that fashion—turn maniacal and run a temperature, hit my head against the wall and end up an opium addict. I begin to get a sense that the future is not Istanbul Avenue straight ahead. There are dark, abysmal back alleys and cul-de-sacs populated by the likes of my uncle and Maryam.

My father's voice brings me back to earth. I go back to the parlor where all my fears and apprehensions dissipate. The windows are open and the sun streams in, lighting up the carpet all the way to the wall. The drapes have recently been washed, giving off the smell of starch and whitener, the smell of cleanliness and health. My thoughts turn to Maryam who is free, wherever she may be now. I decide I would do the same as she did under the circumstances. The thought empowers me and I am possessed with a sense of brute physical strength. I can even wrestle with my brother and subdue him. I stride triumphantly into the hall where I see my cousin, Auntie Azar's elder son, leaning against the doorjamb. He is an obnoxious, filthy brat, who some time ago stole my marbles and the bell off my bike. He is two years older than I and has a thick neck. I look into his eyes and see in them some resemblance to my uncle's, reflecting the same bullying self-centeredness. I clench my fist and hit him straight in the nose. The force of the blow knocks his head against the wall and makes him cry in pain. He is so taken aback that he remains immobile. I kick him in the shin as I go past him back to the parlor and to my father's presence. He laughs and I share in his mirth.

The marriage vows will be exchanged tomorrow afternoon. In the mean time, we will sleep over at Grandma's. I am the only grandchild allowed to sleep with the grown-ups in the big living room, which is now covered wall-to-wall with mattresses and sleeping gear for the elder ladies of the family. There is Khaleh Khanum with her horse-like features and long neck. She has dyed her hair and eyebrows jet black. As always she is meticulously clean and refrains from touching anything. Mrs. Parsa is dwarfishly small. Her feet dangle when she sits on a chair. She wears pancake make-up, her cheeks glowing with two perfectly round circles of rouge. She chain smokes as she reads newspapers or books. She is the only female intellectual in the family. With my father, she discusses important issues touching the Shah and the British foreign policy. Gohartaj Khanum loves children. She has a dozen of her own. Every time I go past her, she involuntarily reaches out and pats my head, showering me with terms of endearment. I will be sleeping between her and my mother. I am surrounded with all sorts of mothers, grandmothers, and aunts. I am engulfed in the warmth of their affection and good will. I am so wound up that I can't sleep. I am soothed by my mother's gentle breathing and the sweet puffing sounds of the sleeping old women. The only sound that disturbs me is the ticking of the old clock in the hall. Gohartaj Khanum is looking after me. Periodically, she wakes up and pulls the eiderdown over my shoulders. I can smell the aroma of grated almonds and baklava wafting from the kitchen. There is also the smell of tomorrow, my cousin's wedding, mixed with the stench of Madame Ana's rejuvenating skin cream.

The traffic begins early in the morning with the ringing of the doorbell and the telephone. There are the sounds of soft chatter and giggles, the clinking of tea glasses, gurgling of boiling water in the samovar. The bridegroom arrives first, bringing bags full of fruit and confectioneries. He pants and seems harried but at every chance he stops to chat with my cousin, his betrothed, who blushes furiously. Auntie Azar is keenly aware of these interludes. She winks at my mother and smiles.

Next is Hassan Agha, who arrives with his pots and pans and utensils. Resplendent in his new outfit, he takes command of the kitchen and starts issuing orders.

A back room has been designated for the bridal make-up. A brazier of glowing hot coals is next to the wall with a curling iron being heated on it. I too am supposed to have my hair curled.

Auntie Azar works on my cousin's face, removing facial hair by using depilating strings. Later she will wax her legs. My cousin's face is flushed, and there are noticeable welts where hairs have been plucked. In time, my hair is curled and I am dressed up in my new clothes. I am not used to being fussed over so much. I get a little flustered and cranky. I feel like I am someone else, one of those classy, marriageable girls whom every drug addict like my uncle can bully and restrict to quarters.

Guests begin to arrive at mid-day. Soon, the bride is ushered in to the yodeling of Tooba Khanum. The congregation begins to sing the traditional wedding song in chorus. The yard suddenly fills up with children of all sizes and shapes. No sooner has Auntie Azar's little boy arrived than he falls off a wall and blood gushes out of a cut on his head. My other cousins get drenched by the fountain in the middle of the pool. Occasionally, Tooba Khanum emerges from the house, slaps a child in her own brood, and goes back inside. Ghostlike, my uncle watches the proceedings from his perch up on the pump house. His main concern, though, is the neighbor's cat that recently killed a couple of his favorite pigeons.

Upon learning that a supply of sweets, cakes, and cookies is set aside in the hall for us children, we rush in. A large dish of rice cookies is overturned and a scuffle ensues. Grandma appears in the hall and starts thrashing a switch freshly cut from a tree at our bare legs. In the chaos, I am hampered by the long cowl as I try to stand my ground against the boys; and every brat that passes me by feels compelled to pull on the curls in my hair.

In the main reception room, music is playing. My mother has brought the family gramophone and the groom, ostensibly possessed of musical talent, sings what passes for Turkish and Russian songs. He sounds more like the Istanbul Avenue orange vendors.

Because Auntie Azar's daughter and I have had dance lessons at Madame Yelena's academy, we are ordered to perform "classical" dance. A hush falls over the congregation as if in anticipation of an important event in art history. The only noise is the bubbling of Grandma's water pipe, mixed with scratchy sound emanating from the ancient gramophone. I push myself against the wall, absolutely refusing to cooperate. My cousin, on the other hand, after mildly demurring, gets into the act. Like a mechanical toy, she raises her arms above her head and tiptoes to the middle of the room where she pirouettes, runs a few steps, and jumps, a faint attempt at a *pas de bourree*, for which she receives applause. Encouraged, she repeats the routine, this time more spiritedly, so much so that she threatens to overturn the large fruit basket which Grandma saves by grabbing it out of her way. My father, already having lost interest in the exercise, declares, "That's nice." All heads turn to him, effectively terminating the dance event. When my father talks, everyone listens, and when he laughs, so does everyone else.

Gradually, a game of hide-and-seek is initiated by the boys, in which I participate. I hurriedly look for a suitable place to hide. The "it" of the game is counting rapidly. But where do I hide? I suddenly see the staircase leading to the second floor. But that's off-limits to kids, I remind myself. However, with time running out and all nearby places taken up, I bolt up the stairs, briefly pausing on the landing. I have never been here before. The space is cool and quiet, as if miles removed from the *opera buffa* in progress on the lower floor. It feels like another region, another world. I should not be here. I should not be aware of the heartache associated with this place. But I cannot help climbing up the remaining steps. The door to one of the rooms is ajar and I move toward it. Suddenly, those demons are back in my head and forcing me to disobey my mother—and feel excited doing it. "Why shouldn't you know? Why shouldn't you see?" the demons tell me. Misdeeds are inscribed on one's forehead, says my mother.

"Nonsense!" say the demons. "Look, there is nothing on your forehead."

"That writing is invisible to children," counters my mother. "Only grown-ups see it." Perhaps she is right. I feel a burning sensation on my brow as the demons guide my hand toward the doorknob. As the door opens, I see a bed in the corner of the room. Lying on it is not a monster as I had expected, but an exquisitely handsome young man with a shock of long, light-brown hair around his face, a face almost feminine in its delicate features. He is pale and his eyes are closed. I am struck by his long eyelashes. He bears no resemblance to any other of my uncles—or to my father or Hassan Agha for that matter. There is a storybook quality to his appearance, like a spellbound prince imprisoned in a castle. He is completely motionless. Is he sleep? I look closely. He is dead! My heart sinks.

I can hear my playmates downstairs looking for me. I must get away. But I am mesmerized by my uncle's ghastly face. All of a sudden, I am aware of the music and the hubbub of voices from the wedding. Strangely, I find them good, lively sounds.

"Death is a kind of a journey," I recall my mother saying. "There is no cause for grief. Grandpa, Mr. Parsa, and Auntie Akhtar have all gone on this trip."

But this is different from other trips. "When you die," says the all-knowing Tooba Khanum, "you go to another world."

"What other world?" I want to know.

I am brought back to myself as I hear the "it" counting at the foot of staircase. I run downstairs in a mad, headlong dash. I am immediately nabbed and it is my turn to be "it." I start counting, but I am agitated and can't stop thinking of the outstretched figure I saw upstairs. "How is it to be one moment and then not to be?"

Lunch is announced by Auntie Azar. "Kids stand aside," she orders, "and wash your hands."

The bride is still dancing with the groom and she looks ecstatically happy. Even Grandma is beaming with joy, apparently oblivious momentarily of her sons. My father resoundingly announces his readiness for lunch, putting an end to our game and other activities.

I stand at the hall doorway feeling oddly queasy and tremulous. I have seen people die in the moves; they are shot and immediately drop dead. My mother dismisses that as a show, a feigning. Is my uncle upstairs feigning death just to scare me? Is that why my mother does not want me to go upstairs?

I spot Madame Ana among the guests. She is wearing one of the hats she says she has made for Princess Ashraf. Mrs. Parsa is sitting on a chair next to my father's, with her customary newspaper and cigarette.

The clock at the end of the hall chimes loudly. To me, it sounds disturbing and ominous, bringing on a nauseous feeling.

"Lunch," booms my father. He then calls Hassan Agha to indicate his displeasure at the delay. This sends everybody scurrying to set the arrangements. Sounds of frantic activity come from the kitchen. To add to the commotion, Tooba Khanum's grandchild has upset the samovar, spilling boiling water on his leg. Flustered and confused, Tooba Khanum gives him a sound beating.

Suddenly and comically, Auntie Azar breaks out singing the wedding song. In another part of the hall I see my mother laughing jubilantly, perhaps amused by a joke. I have an urge to be near her and hold her hand. My father is now only thinking of eating. Hassan Agha, totally absorbed in the intricacies of serving lunch, has no time for me. Dazed and alienated, I watch the swirl of dishes, spoons, forks, salad bowls, bread baskets, soup tureens, and rice plates. I see people rushing back-and-forth—and hear my mother's interminable laughter.

First, the elderly ladies of the clan are served, with father heading the table. A corridor is opened for the bride and bridegroom to their places. An hour after lunch, the wedding vows will be exchanged.

I am feeling progressively worse.

There is a photographer, and my mother wants me to be with her in the wedding picture. " Smile," she snaps. "Wipe that sour look off your face!" I wish I could tell her what I did and what I saw. If she only looks at me she can read it on my forehead. But she is too busy, too preoccupied with the guests and the food.

Within minutes, the feeding frenzy is in full swing. Somehow, people are changing their shapes and looking different from their former selves. They are twisted, crumpled, and wrinkled.

"There is something wrong with this kid," notes Grandma as she looks at me closely. "She's so pale."

"Your turn will come too," says Tooba Khanum and chuckles ambivalently. I see her mouth is a dark cavern, opening up wider and wider.

"This clock is a hundred-and-fifty years old and will be here after we're all gone." After us. After my father. After me. After my uncle is my turn . . . my turn.

I scream as I drop the plate and break into an uncontrollable fit of sobbing. Everyone turns and looks at me. All faces look hideously distorted with age and disease, even my mother's.

"This child's struck with the evil eye," is Grandma's diagnosis. "Somebody crack an egg," she yells an order to no one in particular.

By now I am in the full grip of one of those howling bouts of crying that my mother hates so much.

In an effort to sooth me, Tooba Khanum embraces me hard.

"It's bile," is Khaleh Khanum's opinion. "Give her some warm sugar syrup."

"You must have had a bad dream last night," my mother tells me. "It's because you don't eat enough," she speculates. "Go lie down for a while."

Taking that as her cue, Tooba Khanum savagely drags me off with her to Grandma's bedroom. The room is in an isolated part of the house at the end of a long corridor. It is sparsely furnished with a narrow bed and a large radio. I crawl under the blanket but feel an internal chill. Perhaps if Grandpa was still living he could do something for me, just as he did for my other uncle over the pump house. I think of his delicious concoctions and how much I loved his shop. I remember the fetus in formaldehyde. He is lucky because he'll never grow up, get married—or die.

The wall clock is somewhere near, I remember. I try to sleep but can't because I am shivering. I close my eyes.

"Tick tock, tick tock, tick tock."

Behind my closed eyelids, I see a distant vision of Istanbul Avenue and the mannequin with the low-neck dress in the clothing store window. I see she is slowly changing into my mother and beckoning to me. I hear Hassan Agha urging me to seek help from the fairies. "Demons make you cry," his voice echoes hauntingly in my head.

Moments later, I hear the door opening, and a sweet aroma reaches my nostrils. It is Gohartaj Khanum. She has brought me a sweetened drink flavored with rose water. She sits by me and strokes my hair. She is so pleasant, like Thursday afternoons, all sweetness and light, a harbinger of good things to come and the fun and games of summer. Thinking of summer warms me up and sets the demons in flight. I touch my face against the back of her hand, and the internal turmoil subsides. Nineteen days before the New Year, and I already smell the scent of ripening fruit coming in through the open window. I feel Gohartaj Khanum's warm breath embracing me and think of bike-riding in nearby streets, Friday-evening strolls in the public square, Bahar movie theater, Vila ice-cream, neighborhood boys, the Shemiran bus, and Istanbul Avenue.

I cuddle against Gohartaj Khanum for security and warmth. My body relaxes and my eyelids droop heavily. In the back of my eyes, a few bubbles of lights dance airily, fairies perhaps romping in my head.

Grandma's house has now been sold and the big wall clock moved to the residence of one of my uncles—the last remaining one. Sometimes, in my head I hear its pernicious ticking, and I am reminded that it will be here "after we are all gone." I always resent the persistence of its revolving hands. But these thoughts are regularly followed by a fresh and sacred fragrance that permeates my room and, like Gohartaj Khanum's soothing touch, takes me back to the frantic and fantastic world of childhood. I have a sense that in this touch there is a timeless message— simple, wholesome, and light as the melodic chants of fairies that drown out the fearsome ticking of all the clocks in the world.

---

[1] In Iran, as in other Islamic countries, Friday is the Sabbath, and the week-end begins at noon on Thursday.

[2] A person bearing an aristocratic title.

[3] "Khanum" is a term respectfully and affectionately applied to older women of some stature in the family. They may include maids and housekeepers of long standing. "Jan" is a term of endearment.

[4] Iranian monetary unit.

[5] The former Shah's twin sister.

[6] A street in the prime shopping district in Tehran until the mid-fifties. Istanbul Avenue is another street in that district.

[7] Iranian New Year begins on the vernal equinox.

Father

It was in our first house on Good Fortune Avenue that my sister died. "We came to misfortune on Good Fortune Avenue," my mother noted. So we pack up and move to Shemiran,[1] to the foothills of Elahieh and the Amanieh boondocks. Acquaintances watch in amazement and whisper their doubts about my father's sanity in one another's ears. After all, Shemiran is at the other end of the world. Yet they trust my father's market intuition because he is a native of Qum.[2] So they all follow us (especially my uncles), and we become neighbors. Right on Pahlavi Avenue, we build a big house complete with a garden and reflecting pool. "This is exactly the house I want. My very own house!" exclaims my father.

My father has designed the house himself. Room after room after room, strung one after another like wagons of a train. Upstairs is the reception parlor. It is reserved for important holidays and special occasions or very important guests. Its windows are sometimes opened and its drapes aired. But more often it is all closed up and its furniture covered by sheets. Hassan Agha's kitchen is the nucleus of the house, its window opening onto the garden and catching a lot of light. Like the temple of the holy fire, it is revered as the source of life and plenty.

The Shemiran house with its bright days and its trees casting mysterious shadows: its magically translucent nights echoing with the deliciously muffled voices of neighborhood boys outside its walls; its moments chuck full of childhood joys and maternal ministrations; its immanent apprehensions and sorrows; its surface benevolence and deep-set malice; its transient revelries and resilient doubts; its dynastic ostentations. It sits under the bluest sky, a fertile uterus, and Father for the hundredth time blurts out, "This is exactly the house I want. My very own house!"

The garden is a menagerie of animal statuary. At the foot of the staircase leading up to the patio, two huge concrete lions with jaws wide open are ready to pounce on the arriving guests. On various spots in the middle of flowerbeds and along the pathways, there are metal cutouts of whooping cranes and skinny, emaciated deer frozen in mid-leap. At the far end of the pool, a chunky mermaid, not unlike Fakhr-Azam Khanum in contour, has raised herself on its gilded tail, balancing a blinking light upon her head.

During the summer, we live in the basement, where it is dark and the air is laden with humidity, making us feel cold and clammy even under the sheets. A dais at one end is reserved for Father. Along one side of the basement, there is a small, mosaic pond, perpetually overflowing and making a bubbling sound. Hassan Agha, the cook, floats canta-loupes and watermelons in the pond to keep them cool. My mother splashes rose water on the reed curtains hanging in the windows, imbu-ing the air with damp fragrance. The siesta is compulsory for everyone in the household (decidedly a hardship for us children). We wear paja-mas and lie side-by-side on thick sheets reeking of starch and bluing. At some distance from the rest and close to the mosaic pond, a mattress is laid for Father with mosquito netting draped over it to protect him from flies. Mother makes sure that he has a restful nap. She sprays insecticide around his mattress and flicks the fly swatter at our bare feet if we make a sound. The hour of freedom is announced when Father opens his eyes. Window shades are rolled up, bedding is gathered, and noises of re-sumed activity begin to rise. Hassan Agha arrives carrying a tray loaded with plates and knives to cut the fruit. He places the first slice of the watermelon in front of Father and watches him with the most meaning-less smile in the world. If the fruit is not ripe and sweet, he is fined two tomans, about thirty cents. Father's punishment is in the form of fines. Everyone in the household is on his payroll–maids, servants, Mother, my brother and I, my aunts, tutors, and some strangers who come to the house at the beginning of each month to collect their pay. Father keeps a record of fines in a scroll and docks our pay at the end of the month for transgressions we might have committed. Hassan Agha and I often end up owing more than our stipend—in which case the balance is debited to the next month's pay. Hassan Agha always grumbles vociferously and threatens to quit. He picks up his bundle of clothes and belongings, heading for the door, but changes his mind as soon as he hears Father's voice. He seems in thrall to Father, giving expression to his submissiveness sometimes by loving words, sometimes with outbursts of temper and outrage. His servility is not a matter of choice and calculation or fear and force. It is irrational and instinctual, as inevitable as the juncture of an object and its shadow, matter and the gravitational force.

The Shemiran house is the axis of the life of the whole clan. As children we grow as fast as the aspens, jolly and carefree, roaming the stretches of the green lawns and the fecund orchard, thinking them unbounded and eternal. I don't think of people as being mortals–least of all myself, my mother, Hassan Agha and others–ensconced as we are under the safety umbrella of Father, the Grand Magician, immune to the slings and arrows of outrageous fortune. "I am steel," Father declares, "and steel never rusts."

He is not too far off the mark either. No one has ever seen him sick. He is iron-willed with nerves of steel and has implicit faith in three things—justice, knowledge, and "modernity"—and thinks of wealth as the means of achieving these and avoiding need, subservience, and covetousness.

Some evenings, when he is in a good mood, Father calls me and my brother to his presence. As he pats my head, his steady, assured hand transmits a mysterious force into me, settling in the recesses of my being, a force handed down from ancient ancestors, like a sacred trust, a hedge against uncertainties and moments of doubt, against despair and days of darkness and gloom that the future might bring.

"What grade are you in?" he always has to ask.

"Seventh," I lie. Actually, I am one grade higher.

"What do you want to be when you grow up?" He has asked me this a hundred times.

"A writer," I answer.

"A smart writer or a show-off poet?" he wants to know.

"A rich writer," I retort, to get him to leave me alone.

He chuckles, apparently with satisfaction. He's told us many times not to count on him when we grow up. He wouldn't give us a penny. Sooner or later we'd be out of the fold in some far corner of the world, studying or working. "The kids must go abroad," he's said many times, "stand on their own feet and make something of themselves." It is in keeping with this philosophy that Mr. Ghazni, the tutor of English, is introduced into our world. As it turns out, we learn a lot of things from him, but English is not among them.

Father comes home one day around lunchtime with this English tutor in tow. He gathers us all around him, taking off his shoes, handing his brief case to Hassan Agha and his coat and tie to Mother. He beckons to the greasy, dark-skinned man standing near the door. "Come in, Mr. Ghazni," he commands in English. We are all standing around staring at the ugly-looking stranger in amazement and exasperation but dare not giggle or ask questions.

Mr. Ghazni looks like a panhandler from India. He is hideous. He has bulging, bloodshot eyes and a flat nose with large, flaring nostrils. His lips are dark. His head is bent down, gazing at the floor. As if he finds the reflection of his ugliness in our eyes, he writhes with embarrassment. A strong body odor mixed with a whiff of an Indian perfume radiates from him. He is conscious of it and, like an animal caught in the midst of predators, looks pleadingly at Father for rescue, casting quick glances at the exit door.

The table is set for lunch, and Father takes his place at the head, pulling his plate before him. Without looking up, he points at Mr. Ghazni. "Come. Sit. Eat," he commands. Like an automaton, Mr. Ghazni moves forward, head still down, and places himself at the very edge of the chair. Acutely aware of the odor he is emitting, he tries to shrink in size to reduce the space he occupies. His hands are like superfluous appendages, which he does not know where to put.

Under orders from father but with utmost reluctance, grumbling disgustedly under his breath, Hassan Agha sets a place for Mr. Ghazni at the table. His body language and facial gestures indicate the sad reality that the Indian stranger in his view is a lower life form, inferior to the Armenian or other foreign tutors. Mr. Ghazni, too, senses the low regard in which he is held by the haughty cook and is duly apologetic and diffident. My brother and I snicker—which is noticed by the Indian. There is a boyish glint in his eyes, which for a fleeting moment offsets his hideousness, as if he wears it like a mask, to hide behind it a simple, lovable face to which only Father is privy. It is only Father who knows the charm hidden inside Mr. Ghazni, just as he knows about the gardens of lovely vegetation hidden from view behind high, cement walls.

"This is your English tutor," announces Father. "Anyone caught speaking Persian to him will be fined." He then turns to Mr. Ghazni and asks in English, "What is your name?" Startled, Mr. Ghazni replies hastily, "My name is Ghazni, Sir."

My brother burst out laughing and again the same boyish glint appears in Mr. Ghazni's eyes. There is something pleasant in his glance, timid and cautious, looking for signs of friendship and fun, longing for small talk and warm relations. I begin to feel that I can trust this odd fellow, that he can be a friend.

Next to the kitchen, there is a storeroom, which is cleaned and furnished with an old rug, a bed, a table, and a lamp for Mr. Ghazni. And thus Mr. Ghazni becomes officially a member of the household and resident of the compound. On Father's orders, he is supplied with a white linen shirts and new trousers. He is given two pairs of Father's old shoes and sent off to the public baths and barber shop to be cleansed, deodorized, and sanitized with all kinds of deodorants, disinfectants, and insecticides. He is also forbidden to wear Indian fragrances. Upon his return, the English tutor smells good and is fully groomed, wearing a broad smile. He comes to the breakfast table and effusively greets us. His greetings, however, are in Persian. He is fined five tomans to be docked from the next month's pay.

When Father is not home, English lessons fall by the wayside. The English tutor is transformed into Hassan Agha's subaltern, assigned all kinds of chores, which he can do skillfully. In the kitchen he cleans rice, vegetables, and beans. When we have company he dons a white jacket and serves tea and refreshments. With a prideful smile, Mother glances at Shokat-A'zam Khanom and the incurably pretentious Fakhrosaltaneh girls, flamboyantly uttering such monosyllables as "come" or "go" in

English, dismissing Mr. Ghazni, the "foreign" valet, with a wave of the hand.

Soon Mr. Ghazni is our playmate and a close follower of Hassan Agha. At night, after things settle down, he tells us about himself and the marvels of his native land, India, of his bravery in the war of independence against the British. His stories amount to volumes and are more engaging than those of *A Thousand and One Nights.* Perhaps he makes them up; perhaps he is a poet with overactive imagination or perhaps a dreamer. Whatever he is, he cheers up the dreary nights (when Mother is not home) at the Shemiran house. Even the supercilious cook, bird-brained and narrow-minded as he is, has stopped shunning Mr. Ghazni and counts him among his friends.

Father's English lessons are at night just before bedtime. He has his own method whereby he memorizes thirty or forty entries from the dictionary, on which Mr. Ghazni tests him. To our ears the words are mysterious, echoing the sounds of a magical world, unfamiliar and giving off a disturbing but fascinating aroma, vaguely hinting of wide, untraversed landscapes well beyond the walls of our family compound. They are penetrating and seductive, suggestive of sibylline promises, insinuating an unauthorized contact, as of a forbidden hand touching a pristine body.

The rapid spread of this language, like a contagion, alarms me, and I feel that its arrival in our household signals the end of the happy, carefree days of childhood and ushers in the uncertainties of the future.

My brother is to be sent to America next year, and then will come my turn. In anticipation of this tantalizing and yet frightening eventuality, the days of the summer come to an end with a wrenching haste. Father has memorized eighty-three pages of the English dictionary.

Mr. Ghazni is given one day a week off to visit his family–about whom we know nothing. He always talks of his past–his early youth and travels around the world—but never of the present. When we ask him, he just gives a blank stare, as if he has difficulty remembering where he is or what he has been doing this past twenty years or so. From one of these furloughs, he comes back an hour late and is duly fined. He looks thinner and more rumpled than usual. He is short of breath and has a cough, which he tries to hide from Mother. Next time he goes, he does not come back for three weeks, sending word that he is sick and, when he does come back he is so changed we hardly recognize him. The dark patches under his eyes frighten us. His cheeks are sunken and his mouth gaping. He evades our eyes and his laughter is more like moaning.

Father gives him extra cash and sends him home to rest. I'll never forget his departure, his hand frozen on the doorknob, his step hesitant. His back is toward us, but his neck is twisted in our direction, gazing at our faces. His mouth is half-open as if he is trying to say something but can't remember what. Eventually, he utters a jumble of words, vaguely denoting gratitude, good will, and farewell in a mixture of English and Persian with a smattering of Urdu. But its message is as clear to us, the children, as Mother's call and Hassan Agha's parroting gibberish. It is the language of silent memories, the English dictionary, echoing that first sentence of his, now etched in our memory: "My name is Ghazni, Sir."

A month passes and no news of Mr. Ghazni. No one knows where he lives. He is hugely missed, as if his absence is the omen of other absences to come, and like a cloud of dust it circulates in the big bright rooms of the Shemiran house. Just before the beginning of winter, his wife appears at the house. She is a shriveled woman with very dark skin, speaking Persian with a thick Indian accent, sobbing as she talks. Mother understands. So does Father. Grown-ups always seem to have foreknowledge of bad things. We go for a visit: Father, the wife, Mahmoud Agha the chauffeur, and I. The dwelling is a long way away, beyond the tenements outside city limits. The yard is cobble-stoned and strewn with junk, empty tar drums, and used tires. The family lives at the end of the yard in a single room that looks like a converted garage. Seven or eight small children of different sizes are standing against the wall huddled together motionless, like figurines. Mr. Ghazni is lying on a mattress in the middle of the room. A brazier of glowing coals is at the head of the bed. A tin bowl is bubbling on the brazier, broadcasting a foul odor. The ceiling light is dim, making us look like ghosts. It is as if we have entered into a different world, the world of the dead and of dark shadows.

Mr. Ghazni is lying on the mattress, semi-comatose. Upon hearing the sound of my father's voice, he revives and makes an attempt to raise himself. He says nothing and his face is covered with beads of sweat.

A single chair is brought for my father. It is broken and rickety. With a napkin, the Indian woman wipes the sweat off her husband's face. The children stay immobile and noiseless. The sick man glances toward me, and I see in his eyes for a brief moment the same old goodness and impetuosity–and the last gleam of life.

Father says something to the driver about getting Dr. Kosari and bends down to touch Mr. Ghazni's forehead. The wife is squatting on the floor next to her husband. No words are spoken, and the only noise is my suppressed, intermittent sobbing.

I find my way back to the car, disturbed and confused. I gape at the darkness outside. It is limitless, engulfing the world like an inky ocean, silent, huge, and ominous.

Father returns, walking slowly, ponderously. He sits in the car, looking fatigued and drained. "This is the end for this little man," he mumbles, "I wonder when our turn will come." And he breaks down weeping soundlessly. I can't believe it. I have never seen Father cry. "I am steel and steel never corrodes!" I recall his bravado. Now he weeps and that frightens me. But it is a peculiar fear, a feeling I have never experienced before, for which I have no name. It is an aching sensation that is not in the body; it is in the air, in the universe, in the darkness outside. It is a communal wound afflicting all—Mother, Mr. Ghazni, Hassan Agha, Shokat-A'zam Khanom, everyone in the world. Even the super-rich, and the beautiful models in fashion magazines, even the Shah.

That night I dream of Mr. Ghazni. He is walking in snow barefoot, happy and playful, skating on icy patches. Father is there too with my grandmother. No one feels cold in that field of snow. Where is that? I wake up in a cold sweat. It is a bad dream, it is a dream of dead people. Why is Father there? His words echo in my head: "I wonder when our turn will come."

"Never," I reassure myself. Father is of steel and indestructible. He hates grouches, malingerers, freeloaders, ne'er-do-wells, and fancy-pants. I recall his hectoring: "These young donkeys must work, work, work;

must make something of themselves, stand on their own feet. They must struggle, wrestle, and win." Just as he himself has been doing all his life. "When I left Qum, I did not have a farthing to my name," he has reminded us many times. "But I had the brain and the guts to begin from square one. And here I am today. Don't come to me; I won't give you a penny."

When did Father's sudden illness begin? When did Death knock on the door of the Shemiran house? I don't recall. In the midst of ensuing chaos, those unthinkable transpositions and cataclysms, time does not have its usual meaning and is no longer divisible by day, night, hours, and minutes. It is as if the ultimate "moment" is upon us, that moment of mystery, replete with emptiness, brimming with darkness and silence, that soundless, motionless, eternal minute, beyond the minutes of existence, of history, of life.

No one knows what day of the week and what season of the year it is. We are oblivious to the rising and setting of the sun, the moon, the stars. We don't think of our yesterdays and measure the future only by the irregular rhythm of Father's breathing.

Father's illness takes everyone by surprise, even himself. We all think it is a passing phase, that his steely constitution will pull through unscathed. The illness descends upon the household like an unwelcome visitor—vile, blunt, and aggressive—imposing itself upon Father, spelling usurpation and destruction. The process begins with a small lesion in the foot and its poison spreads the swelling and infection to beneath the knee. Gangrene! A word we have not heard before and non-existent in our vocabulary of daily ailments. Only Mother knows what it means and what danger it poses to the tribal chief. Others are confused and irresolute, wallowing in a shadowy, primal fear. This death, if it comes, is different from others. This is the snapping of the steel rod, the end of an epoch, the collapse of a tradition.

Father loathes hospitals, doctors, and drugs and wants to be home to work, to write the editorials, the legal briefs. He ignores the monstrously swollen leg—and our anxious looks and trembling hands. He thinks of the future, as far away as the next ten years, as if he does not need the leg. He could do with one leg, one hand, one eye and still work,

work for its own sake. He has the obsession of a crazed mountaineer, compulsively climbing simply because those high peaks are there. He laughs at my tears. "Do you remember," he asks rhetorically, "what I said about steel?"

When I look at his face, my fears dissipate: the same gleaming eyes, penetrating and brimming with intelligence, prominent nose, high and jutting forehead. The same hands, criss-crossed with veins. The same gaze, sullen, indifferent, and self-assured.

The Shemiran house is spiritless and cold and the winter harsh and implacable. Under the cover of snow, the figure of the mermaid in the yard looks like an old, bent-over woman. Neighbors, curious, and astonished, wearing looks of false sympathy, step aside as we pass. Deep in their eyes, there is the glint of old jealousies. The breakdown of the "man of steel" is a sort of a vindication for them, the victory of chaff over grain.

Snow falls incessantly, and I dream of Father every night, waking up in expectation of bad news. Doctors, who have already given us the worst-case prognosis, are irritated by Father's resilience and his refusal to succumb. Soon, death is in retreat and Father, vigorous and in high spirits, returns home—minus one leg. He walks even steadier than before on the prosthetic he was fitted with at the hospital and uses the walking stick to snap at Hassan Agha's legs. No sooner has he arrived home than he fines Morteza the Gardener.

The Shemiran house is alive again. Hasan Agha'a kitchen, after a hiatus of quiet, is now a den of activity. Pots and pans are brought out of cabinets and the halls are awash once more with the jingle of glasses and jangle of silverware. A procession of uncles arrives with bouquets of flowers, and neighbors with perfunctory smiles plastered on their lips stop by to offer felicitations. It is as if we have survived the devastation of an earthquake and life rules again over the domain of inanimate objects and dictates the chronology of events.

Every night, with caution and respect bordering on religious reverence, Hassan Agha detaches the prosthetic from Father's stump and gently lays it by the bedside. He does not understand that this is not a part of Father's anatomy. He makes no distinction between his live tissue and his personal effects (shoes, hat, stick, suit, and robe). Whatever belongs to Father is, like him, endowed with a vital and mysterious force, fearsome and dangerous, and yet curative and salutary, much like the wax figurines of an ancient magician capable of interfering with people's destiny. This is what Hassan Agha understands and what he solemnly believes.

With the coming of spring we heave a sigh of relief and celebrate. A picnic is organized in the family estate in Karaj, and we children stuff ourselves to the point of sickness with cherries and plums not quite ripe to eat. But soon, before we are over the episode, Father is under attack by sickness again. This time his eyes are the target. The next round of worries, anxieties, muttered words, doubtful looks, unanswered questions begins anew. Once again we experience interminable seconds and are deep in the black hole of despair. We entertain muddled thoughts of the absolute worst. Lo and behold, there is yet another miracle! Father returns home, this time minus one eye. But the remaining eye is even more penetrating and observant than before, a hundred times more so than the cautious and fearful eyes of others around him.

Uncles arrive again with (this time smaller) flower arrangements, and neighbors, baffled and sullen, drop in to wish Father good health. Hassan Agha, resurrected from a virtual sleep of death, picks up his large shopping bag and heads for the market, comes back with supplies and begins to cook. He stuffs himself and others with food. It is only within Father's magnetic field that his existence has any reality and his identity as the "Old Cook" has any meaning.

Father has plans to build several subdivisions and expand his business emporium. He seems to be rushed, avidly grabbing every moment and minute to push ahead with the work. The Shemiran house, like a city having just emerged victorious from under a heavy siege, is full of energy and renewed life. It looks as if it has reestablished the old order, and Father's law rules supreme over the household. But in the midst of all the excitement, there is a sense that a small cog in this apparatus is out of whack and that there is a menacing darkness flying in the bright, sun-lit rooms of the house, sometimes touching the quivering skin of our anxious faces with its awesome wing-tips.

Death is sitting in ambush behind the hedgerows in the back of the garden, and in the dark of one night mounts its attack–now directly against Father's heart. The sickness and the patient are once again engaged in mortal combat like two old adversaries. And we once again descend into the abyss of despair, watching, helplessly and with bated breath, Father's desperate but no less determined struggle against annihilation.

Destiny, exasperated and frustrated by Father's almost superhuman resiliency, takes another tack. Unable to defeat him in death, it takes aim at his dwelling, his seat of power, the Shemiran house. A major thoroughfare, sumptuously named Imperial Parkway, has been ordained to run from one end of town to another. The Shemiran House sits directly in its path and must therefore be demolished. We are given ten days to vacate—at a time when Father is on his way to Europe—and the rest of us are too feeble to mount a resistance. If Father had not decided to leave, perhaps we could have saved the house. But we are too dazed and disoriented to be effective. Hassan Agha, frightened and in tears, closes down the kitchen, and Morteza the Gardener sorrowfully surrenders the graceful aspens and shady maples to the wrecking crew and leaves.

At a little distance from the house in a narrow and unpaved alley, Father owns a small apartment. That is where we take refuge, in anticipation of Father's return, for which we don't hold out much hope any way.

The demolition day arrives. We wonder if this is a bad dream. Or perhaps the Shemiran house was a dream from which we have now wakened. What we thought was a structure of steel crumbles with a flick of a finger. A thick cloud of dust like the fiery breath of a gargantuan monster engulfs the flowerbeds and manicured lawns. The house itself, with all its ostentation and showy adornments, slips out of sight like an evanescent memory. The mermaid holding the light over her head drowns in a sea of debris and is no more. Like a bubble, Hassan Agha's kitchen bursts and is soon no more than a cloud of dust particles. With its destruction are erased like faint pencil marks the memories of tasteful old delicacies, simple pleasures, and sweet smells that emanated from it during the years of childhood.

Father, barely alive and visibly exhausted but once more victorious over the old adversary, returns. He looks at the empty space that was once the Shemiran house. He registers no protest or regret. He is calm and unperturbed. His silence is more hurtful to me than his old ranting cantankerousness.

We have the money to buy another house elsewhere, build even a bigger kitchen, and plant better trees, but Father is not thinking along those lines. Perhaps he has accepted the fact that his time has expired and the Shemiran house is a thing of the past. He is balanced and indifferent. You win some and you lose some, he seems to say. He is still able to sleep calmly and for long hours. He is asleep before his head hits the pillow, as if he has no care in the world. He no longer has the zeal to fight or the drive for triumph. He has done his work and is no longer beholden to himself, to us, or to the world in general.

It is in this modest and sparsely furnished apartment that he dies, quietly and serenely. This time, death arrives not as the old, invasive adversary but by invitation, peaceably and on time, like a favorite brother arriving from a long journey after many years. Everyone is reconciled to this event, even Mother, even the uncles. And of course the neighbors, the new ones, who can barely hide their smugness. The only person in denial is Hassan Agha. He is not easily accepting of this departure, which to him is unreasonable. He bawls at the head of Father's deathbed and then hastily packs his meager belongings and departs, furious, resentful, and inimical.

Years later, after the Revolution, Hassan Agha lodges a formal complaint with the authorities against the family and makes sure that we hear about it. "Can you believe it?" blurts out Mother, wounded and heart-broken, "Hassan Agha, the old faithful cook!" I can believe it but don't understand why others don't see that the complaint actually took shape years before, on the day when his kitchen fell victim to the wrecker's ball. That was when Hassan Agha defected from our camp.

It was during the war with Iraq that I ran into him. I am standing by the side of the parkway, more or less on the spot where the Shemiran house was, now a public thoroughfare full of people, cars, horse-drawn carts, and donkey trains passing through what used be its rooms, lawns, and arboretum, and where the light-bearing mermaid lies buried deep in memories.

Hassan Agha, the eternal cook, the keeper of the fire—and the broth—passes by, and his glance, frozen and vacuous, glides over me. He hasn't changed—the same face, the same shock of long greasy hair (now tinged with grey), the same mouth (open but wordless), the same mindless smirk.

A small cab stops, and he takes the seat near the window, looking straight ahead. But then he turns and stares at me for a brief moment. His eyes open wide and his jaw drops. His face glows with recognition. I am sure of that. His breath condenses on the window and hides his eyes. But even before that, for a fraction of second, a glimpse of deep ambiguity, direct and yet paradoxical, bitter and yet conciliatory, finds reflection in his eyes. This glance is laden with a thousand pictures: the old Shemiran bus on its long trek past the snow covered maples of Pahlavi Avenue; the large kitchen well-stocked with pots, pans, and groceries, full of steam and smoke and redolent with smells of family recipes; Father's penalties and fat New-Year tips; Tooba Khanum, the nanny, and her stories populated with genies and fairies; deaths, funerals, and weddings and the tug on the arm of the rambunctious little girls when crossing the street; the nights of religious holidays and concomitant silence and gloom; the bright days of the Shemiran house and happy games; the image of Father, full of contradictions–chieftain of the tribe and grand wizard– and the law of gravity; and a myriad of remembrances, far and near . . .

---

[1] Now a suburb of Tehran, Shemiran used to be a substantial town about thirty kilometers from the capital.

[2] People from central Iran are believed to be astute in matters of commerce.

72

The Maid

When the revolution came, those who worked for us simply got up and left, even Hassan Agha, the cook, who had been with us some forty odd years, and his wife, Zahra Khanum, who always swore we were the apple of her eye, and Morteza the Gardener, who at each prayer heartily blessed Father and everyone in the family–and even Nanny Karaji, who had grown old in our household and was an integral part of it.

With the departure of the old cook, a part of our family history was wiped out—all those memories that involved him: Friday family luncheons, New Year's charity dinners, the pleasing mix of aromas wafting from jars of tomato paste and preserves and condiments in the upstairs pantry, the soothing jangle of dishes and pots and pans, the magical taste of home-cooked meals, and the seemingly unassailable security of the kitchen. With him and Nanny Karaji leaving us, the Shah skipping the country, the uncles hastily migrating to far-off corners of the world, a neighbor's house being confiscated, and Shamsolmoluk Khanum being accidentally "martyred," a door was being forever closed on our past. It was the end of an era and the beginning of something new, something ambiguous, vague, unfamiliar. The logic of daily events escaped us, and history, like the onslaught of a foreign horde, swept away old customs and pillaged what was left of the mythic vestiges of our remembrances. We were left with an assortment of unmatched pieces that did not fall into any recognizable patterns.

Hassan Agha disappeared suddenly and surreptitiously–no goodbyes, no reasons or excuses for leaving. We thought he had been taken ill or–God forbid–had died in one of the clashes of the revolution. We could not imagine that he had left of his own volition until his sons turned up as local revolutionary-committee[1] henchmen and began sending threatening messages. Zahra Khanum, too shy and diffident for a face-to-face encounter, sent an emissary to let us know of the complaint she was filing against us with the authorities.

We could hardly believe any of this. We should talk to Hassan Agha, we decided. Mother and I got dressed and headed for his residence. Nobody answered the door, although we could hear someone inside and see a pair of eyes watching us from behind a curtain in a window. Embarrassed and humiliated, we turned back. In the alley we ran into Morteza the gardener, who turned his head and did not acknowledge us.

We were alone and helpless in a cold and spiritless house. During the power outages at night, we sat around the oil lamp and held our breath in fear any time there was a knock on the door. The younger ones in the family were planning to leave, heading out for Europe, but were concerned about the older folks who would not hear of leaving, nor could they be left behind to fend for themselves. Grandparents, though decrepit and handicapped, had no intention of dying any time soon. Parents, younger but unwilling to migrate and change their life style, dreaded loneliness, revolution, and war. Uncle Colonel was already on the lam, and his mother could not sleep at night, fearing imminent famine and looting. Auntie Malak was afraid of the Afghan wetbacks and was sure they would cut her head off. She would pass a trembling finger across her double-chinned throat, as if feeling the sharpness of the knife in her plump flesh. She would moan in an agony of fear. My physician uncle, surpassing all in wisdom, got himself a pair of grown dogs, German shepherds both (which immediately proceeded to bite Mother on the thigh and my aunt on the ankle), installed several alarms and early warning systems, and hired a security guard to watch him and the house.

Mother was hurt mostly by Hassan Agha's desertion. She never mentioned his name but could not forget him either. She insisted on hiring a new servant mostly to assuage her wounded pride. But how could we bring a stranger into the house? How could we trust a stranger in this day and age? I was planning to leave, and war was about to break out. I had to find a trustworthy person to care for Mother. Mohammad Agha, the neighborhood carpenter, had a reputation for being a solid and decent man. We had known him for twenty years and had learned to count on him. He was different from others. I broached the matter with him when he was in the house changing the locks. I told him I was looking for a smart and trustworthy person to look after my mother, and the reason I was talking to him was that my brother the engineer trusted his judgment and had good things to say about him. I was almost certain he would not be interested, finding excuses to deflect the rapprochement. Surprisingly though, he jumped at the suggestion. "With pleasure," he said, as he put down his saw. "I am beholden to your family and the engineer. His wish is my command."

I could not believe it. People promise things but never carry through. I looked at him doubtfully. "Do you know someone trustworthy?" I asked. "I mean, like yourself?"

"Do you think I would recommend an unsuitable person to the service of the Grand Lady?' he said, somewhat miffed. "These days," he continued, "one is suspicious of one's own shadow. I had heard about Hassan Agha and was embarrassed by his behavior. Sincerely, I could not look the engineer in the eye. What a world this has turned out to be! Even a dog does not recognize his master. But we are obligated to you and the Grand Lady's kindnesses. Believe me, my mother blesses the engineer every night at prayer. If she finds out that the Grand Lady needs help, she would volunteer herself."

I thought he was buttering me up. Mohammad Agha, an observant man, read the look of skepticism on my face and took up the issue directly. "I will go right now to my aunt's house," he said resolutely, "and, with her permission, fetch her daughter to attend the pleasure of the Grand Lady."

This was ideal, exactly the person we had in mind. It did not matter whether she could cook, sew, or keep house. The important thing was that she was Mohammad Agha's cousin and, thus, reliable. She would alleviate Mother's concerns and introduce some degree of order in our disrupted lives.

Mohammad Agha explained that his cousin had never worked anywhere and was mostly a homebody, shy and withdrawn, religious and chaste. In other words, she was exactly the person we were looking for. I was only afraid that her mother might oppose the deal. As an added incentive, I let Mohammad Agha know that there would be something in it for him. He rejected the idea with a vehement shake of his head and waving of his hand–which left me somewhat mortified for thinking along those lines.

Mohammad Agha left on his mission, and I rushed home to bring the good news to Mother. Nothing could top this.

At the house, I did not see Hassan Agha himself, but his wife and the bevy of his brood were there, lined up in the corridor near the entrance. Zahra Khanum, trying to be inconspicuous, was standing behind the sons. She held her head down, and the black *chador*[2] covered half her face. The sons were nervous and ill-at-ease, mumbling incoherently. It was the son-in-law who was in control of the mission. We did not know him well, but he certainly was in command.

They wanted money–half the house, part of the garden. Somehow, they knew that legally and in practical terms they had not a leg to stand on; so every time Mother cast ferocious glances in their direction or made a biting remark, they blushed and retreated. There was only one thing certain: neither side was in the same position as in the old days. Shy and maladroit, Zahra Khanum took it upon herself to point this out. From where she stood, she jutted her head and squealed in her high-pitched voice, "So why was there a revolution?" Good question, we all thought.

Going directly to the heart of the matter, my brother asked, "How much do you want?" This took the men by surprise and made them even more inarticulate. Zahra Khanum, holding a corner of the chador in her teeth, batted her trachoma-damaged eyelids uncontrollably. The son-in-law, less mindful of us, blurted out a figure, which in his view was exorbitant. For us, however, it was less than expected. We agreed and the meeting ended abruptly.

The anticipated arrival of a new maid and Mohammad Agha's agency in the matter seemed to soften the blows we had just suffered. "To spite Hassan Agha," Mother intoned, "I will give this girl a higher salary; I'll give her the upstairs room; I'll personally find her a suitable husband..."

I interrupted her and urged her to hold off her munificence until later. But she was excited and on a roll: "The old, stupid, ungrateful jackass. When he came to us he had not even done his national service and did not have a penny to his name. He arrived barefoot from Arak,[3] and I sent him to adult literacy classes. When he brought his diseased, trachoma-stricken cousin from the village, I spent so much on her medical bills that I even paid for his children's schooling. I put together a dowry richer than my own for his daughter's wedding. Now they have the gall to ask 'What was the revolution for?'"

An hour later Mohammad Agha arrived with his cousin. She was young and fresh-faced, rather plump but in a pleasant way. She was wearing a chintz chador but no stockings. Mohammad Agha saw me stare at her bare legs and said quickly, "Forgive her improper appearance. I just picked her up and brought her over. My aunt was not home. She was going to put on black stockings, but I was afraid it might take too long. So I told her to get going."

"We are not strangers any more," said Mother, "but I wish she'd come with the approval of her mother."

"In fact," rejoined Mohammad Agha expansively, " *you* are Zeynab's mother. We are all your servants."

Zeynab lifted her head and stared quizzically at Mother. She then chuckled, returning her gaze to the floor.

" If memory serves, my son had always spoken highly of your aunt. She is a respectable lady."

I knew Mother had never met the woman, but she was so excited that she had convinced herself of the truth of her statement, convinced that the aunt was exactly the kind of person she expected her to be.

We sat on the verandah, and Mother, in a convivial mood, struck up a conversation with Mohammad Agha, asking about his family and making complimentary comments about his wife (although she had never set eyes on her). It looked like she was trying to delay negotiations about Zeynab, relishing the pleasure of the moment like a tasty morsel of food in her mouth. She steered the conversation to the inflationary spiral of prices, shortages of water and electricity, my brother's run-in with the authorities and his recent incarceration, the theft of Uncle Doc's car, and Hassan Agha's traitorous defection. If the conversation continued along these lines, I decided, it would lead to some sensitive issues. So I interrupted her and asked Mohammad Agha to tell us about Zeynab.

"Sit down, dear girl," said Mother. " You'll get tired standing up. Think of this as your own home and of me as you own mother." She then stood up, walked to the fruit basket, piled a plate with fruit, and offered it to Mohammad Agha. Zeynab, who had been standing all this time, sat on a chair at Mother's insistence.

"This girl has never worked anywhere," Said Mohammad Agha. "She is exceedingly naive and simple. My aunt too is old-fashioned and religious. She has made this girl into a true homebody."

"That is how it should be," declared Mother, eying Zeynab with approval. Zeynab dropped her head down and gave a child-like, meaningless giggle, every inch an ingénue, inexperienced with the ways of the world.

"As a matter of fact," Mohammad Agha continued solemnly, "the parents of this poor child died in a car crash when she was barely two months old. She herself was tossed out of the car window, and it was only by divine providence that she was spared. My aunt, devout and Godly as she is, raised this child as if her own. She is the apple of her eye!"

Mother, casting a pitiful eye in her direction, announced, "I will personally watch over her . . . find her a husband. They could live in the cottage at the end of the garden. The husband could work in my son's office. If they had children that proved studious, I'd pay for their education . . . send them abroad."

An agreement was reached soon, and Mohammad Agha, in something of a hurry, rushed out of the house. But before he left, he made two firm provisos: Zeynab was not to be allowed to leave the house under any circumstances—on her days off, the aunt would come for her—and she was not to make or take phone calls.

Mother nodded vigorously in agreement. "Yes, of course," she said, "all these restrictions are absolutely necessary, what with this girl being so young and pretty. You may trust her with me."

Zeynab put away her bundle and took off her chador. "I'll begin from here," she declared, as she cast her glance around the kitchen. She then grabbed a broom, opened the windows, piled the chairs on the table, and began to sweep.

"There you are," I told Mother. "That's a maid for you!"

"What a gem!" replied Mother, ecstatically. She immediately remembered Mohammad Agha's injunctions and told Zeynab that first she should say her mid-day prayers. Zeynab was fully engrossed in her work, beads of perspiration forming on her brow, the thin fabric of her dress sticking to her pale skin, outlining her young, firm flesh. She ignored Mother's bidding, mumbling something about work being more important. This thrilled Mother. Even my suggestion that we should first eat something fell upon deaf ears.

By now Zeynab had moved the cupboards, the refrigerator, and other kitchen furniture and was cleaning the space behind them.

"This is what I call an immaculate, sensible person!" Mother proclaimed. "The important thing is to clean everything, even what is not visible. That filthy Zahra Khanum only passed a hand over things and let it go at that." Mother was now fuming. "And that good-for-nothing husband of hers, Hassan Agha, just eating and sleeping and malingering. Good Riddance! To hell with them!"

Zeynab's dress was deemed short and too open at the neck. We decided to get her a smock and thick hoses. Mother suggested that she wear a light headscarf when we had company. At this suggestion, Zeynab cast an amused glace at us and gave a laugh—which struck me as incommensurate with her look of shy innocence. We postponed lunch until she finished cleaning up the kitchen.

"It is cleaning the nooks and crannies that counts," said Mother. "See how everything shines! This girl is a godsend, an angel. I will take care of her myself–find her a husband, set her up in the lodge at the end of the garden, and have her children sent to America. And if her husband knows something about driving and gardening, he will be the chauffeur and gardener. Forget about that ungrateful Morteza–filing a complaint against us. Imagine! One hair on this girl's head is worth a hundred like that scumbag."

All in all, Zeynab was too good to be true, and with this realization came a certain amount of concern. "Makes me sick to think she may not stay," said Mother, her face etched with worry. "She is young and gullible. Neighbors will get her away from us. We are finished if your Auntie

Malak finds out about her. Mustn't praise her a lot. With such shortage of good help, she'll be whisked away in no time."

A knock on the door brought our hearts to our mouths. It was Mohammad Agha.

"Miss, he is here to take you home, I guess," I suggested to Zeynab.

"To hell with him," she blurted out, with one hand at her hip, glowering at the doorway. "Still a free country, isn't it?"

Mother cast a surprised and confused glance in my direction. The bewilderment in her look shot through me. There was something grating and strident in Zeynab's voice that ran counter to her diffident, peasant-like smile.

It so happened that Mohammad Agha had come to collect his tools. We asked him to stay for lunch but he declined. He was in hurry to get somewhere. Before he left, though, he took Zeynab aside and talked to her under his breath. Like an impetuous, playful child, Zeynab shifted from foot to foot, scratched her upper thigh, and rolled her eyes with impatience.

"The more advice she gets the better," noted Mother. "There is good reason to be concerned." No sooner had Mohammad Agha left than Zeynab returned to her cleaning zealously, as if her life depended on it. Despite her small stature, she was amazingly strong, easily moving heavy furniture around. "Dear girl," pleaded Mother apprehensively, "don't move that antique vase, please. It might shatter. No need to dust the china. Please leave the crystal chandelier alone." It was no use. Stubbornly, Zeynab proceeded with her task, ignoring Mother's pleas. Eventually we gave up and left her to her own devices. Although she insisted on total obedience from the household staff, Mother watched Zeynab with obvious satisfaction as she went through the house bestowing a sheen of cleanliness on everything she touched.

She finished around two in the afternoon. Not feeling hungry, she pushed her food aside and drank a whole bottle of water. She then washed her face and wetted her hair in the sink, plumped down in the middle of the living room floor and went out like a light. Perspiration oozed from her pores, and an animal warmth radiated from her young, firm, healthy flesh. The short skirt was riding up her thighs, revealing a glimpse of her flowered underwear. She looked younger in her sleep, with her pink cheeks and turned-up eyelashes. Something primitive and amorphous in her body coupled with that impish, sensual smile, imbuing her child-like presence with ambiguity and suggestiveness.

In the early evening the telephone rang. It was Mohammad Agha's aunt who wanted to talk to Mother about Zeynab. I listened to the conversation from the extension in my bedroom. The woman sounded more literate and cultured than expected from a peasant. She said she worked in an office, knew of our family, and had a nodding acquaintance with my father whom she admired. Getting to know my mother would be a great honor, she added. She had also heard good things about my brother and me and believed Zeynab to be exceptionally lucky to have ended up in our household. She mentioned, sort of off-hand, that Zeynab had many suitors, and it was possible that some of them might try to talk her into marriage, something she would not allow, nor would she allow her to talk to any men.

Profusely, Mother assured her that Zeynab's virtue would be protected at all costs and, at the proper time, she would herself find her a suitable husband, send her children to school, etc., etc., etc. Reassured, the woman hung up and we all felt that we now had a reliable housemaid on a permanent basis. I even fantasized about taking trips, certain that Mother was securely ensconced in her home with adequate help. My brother, too, would rest at ease, once he heard the good news, thanking God for this piece of good fortune.

The dusk had barely fallen when Auntie Malak arrived at our house. Her eyes popped at the sight of Zeynab. "Where did this come from?" she exclaimed. Mother tried to shrug it off. She said casually that the girl was a relative of Mohammad Agha, the carpenter, that she was not much good and completely untrustworthy. The last epithet shook up Auntie. "She is not Afghani, is she?" she asked apprehensively. Mother hunched her shoulders, shook her head, and curled the corners of her mouth as a gesture of uncertainty. "What? Are you crazy?" Auntie exploded, raising her hand to her throat. "If she is Afghani, you're gonna be done with tonight! How stupid! Where did you get her, any way?"

Mother was being obnoxious, of course, while I was trying to calm Auntie down. But she wasn't to be comforted, casting suspicious glances at Zeynab. "I'd rather die a death of loneliness, wash floors, and clean house by myself than let a stranger into my life," she announced. "Just the night before last they raided the home of an elderly couple and cut their heads off. That's what the papers said. It is the work of Afghanis, they say. Same thing with Mrs. Khavary. They gagged her in her kitchen and beat her on the head with a club. They tie up the kids and twist their necks like chickens."

Zeynab brought in the tea tray. Mother looked at her pridefully and said, "Zeynab is every inch a lady, and I am happy with her." As she picked up the empty glasses, Zeynab turned and looked at Mother with a grin and murmured, "Don't count your chickens before they're hatched!"

I couldn't believe my ears. Mother gave a hollow laugh, trying to look as if she hadn't heard it. But Auntie, on full alert, heard everything and let her jaw drop. "Did you hear that? Don't count your chickens. . . What gall, the little bitch!" she exclaimed.

Desperate for a way out, Mother groped for words. She said dismissively, "Ah, you blow things out of proportion, Auntie. She just said something. Not that she has any education. Perhaps she just wanted to be complimentary. The end is always better than the beginning."

Auntie was not to be comforted. She was worried, most of all for my brother. "What if she reports on us?" she speculated.

Mother, frustrated and irritable, gulped down her tea. "So what? We haven't done anything. What have we to be afraid of? We have nothing to hide," she said firmly.

At this point, Auntie rose to her feet and straightened the large scarf covering her head, pulling it almost down to her eyes. "You must protect yourself," she advised. "Just the fact that you're sitting here hale and hearty is itself a crime. Our crime is that we still have our heads on our shoulders. What's worse?"

When Auntie departed, Mother and I felt ill at ease. We began reading the afternoon papers with a bad taste in our mouth because of Auntie's blabbering. Mother stood up, looking around indecisively, as if she wanted to say something but had changed her mind. She sat down again.

By this time Zeynab had finished her work. She sidled toward me, craning to see the pictures in the paper. "These are all dead?" she asked.

"Let me see," interrupted Mother, "have you recited your evening prayers? Mohammad Agha was very particular about that, you know." Ignoring her, Zeynab pointed to the paper. "What's written in there?" she asked, her curiosity piqued. When the telephone rang, she jumped. "I'm sure it is for me!" she chirped, as she reached for it. Mother blocked her advance, yelling "Wait a minute, girl!" as she picked up the receiver. "Hello, hello," she repeated into the phone, but there was no answer.

"I told you it was for me," said Zeynab defiantly. Mother, trying to control her temper, replied, slowly and deliberately, "You must never pick up the phone. Your aunt insists on it. Do you understand?" There was so much authority in her voice that even I was transfixed. Zeynab, pale and intimidated, gathered herself and lowered her eyes. "I'm going to water the flowers," she said timidly. But then she turned to me and like an excited child talking to a playmate asked, pointing to the newspaper, "What's written here? Are they dead? Must have been smugglers, right?" Without waiting for an answer, she careened down the stairs, picked up the garden hose, and turned on the tap. She took off her slippers, splashing water on her feet. She exuded the freshness of a flower patch, and her youth, like the fragrance of acacia vine, permeated the yard. She was childlike in her joyousness, making it hard not to excuse her occasional odd behavior and words. Mother was once again well-disposed, forgetting the Auntie's injunctions. Her face glowed with a halo of satisfaction as she peeled an apple and shared it with me.

Our neighbor's servant, we noticed, was standing on the roof. "Look at that son of a bitch," Mother noticed, "ogling at my girl."

"Hey mister," she whooped, " what are you standing there for, feasting your eyes? Don't you know you can't invade folks' privacy? Get down or I am calling the Committee right now." The man snickered and shrugged his shoulders. "It is your own fault—your gallivanting in the yard unveiled. If you had any modesty you'd cover yourselves," he said.

"Can't we breathe free in our own house?" Mother wanted to know. She picked up her tea glass and turned to Zeynab. "Come on in, missy," she said. "From now on, don't get out there without a head cover."

I felt drained and listless. Without a word I picked up my books and newspaper and went inside. Zeynab squatted next to me, mumbling. Suddenly she said, "I just want to talk."

I ignored what she said and continued reading. She said again, "I know I am not supposed to talk, but I really want to talk."

"All right, go ahead and talk," said Mother impatiently. "What do you want to talk about?"

"I'm scared Mohammad Agha will cut my head off."

"You get up and get ready for your prayers. Don't think bad thoughts," commanded Mother. "Mohammad Agha is harmless," she said.

Zeynab got quiet and thoughtful. It was obvious she was dealing with some kind of an internal conflict. Absent-mindedly, Mother was thumbing through the pages of a magazine when the telephone rang again but stopped before we picked it up. Standing motionless, Zeynab raised her hand to her face to hide an amused sneer. I looked at her, an ominous feeling going through me. Her behavior was certainly bizarre. She noticed I was staring at her. "What are you reading?" she asked, taking her hand off her face.

I held the book in front of her and asked, "How many grades have you finished?" Mother, not waiting for an answer, interjected, "My girl, I can put you in adult literacy classes, if you want. Mohammad Agha said you have finished elementary school."

"I have a question," said Zeynab, changing the subject. "You are all so educated and understand everything so well. Just tell me how it is possible for two grown people to die in a car crash but an infant get thrown out through the windshield without a scratch."

Mother and I exchanged glances. Deep in my heart I had a sense that trouble was ahead. Mother frowned with a certain look in her eyes. She pursed her lips, and deep lines appeared in the corners of her month.

"You are so naive," Zeynab persisted. "I'll be skinned alive if Mohammad Agha finds out I have opened my mouth. But you are so nice; I just can't lie to you."

The doorbell rang. It was the sanitation man calling for a spot of lunch and his monthly allowance. We were left alone again after his departure. I pulled Zeynab aside and told her that talk like that disturbs Mother. "But I swear on the Koran I am not lying," she protested. This woman who claims to be Mohammad Agha's aunt is lying. I don't know who my parents are. For all I know I may be a foundling."

As she turned towards us, Mother heard the last sentence. Color drained from her face. "Do you realize," she said sternly, "that if you lie, all your prayers will be nullified?"

Zeynab laughed pejoratively. "Oh, come on, who says I pray? Mohammad Agha's aunt has never said a prayer in her life, and he himself a drunk with no religion!"

Mother was almost in shock. "Look here," she warned, "I'm going to call her and tell her what you're saying behind her back"

"I don't care," said Zeynab, pouting. "She'll come and get me and throw me in the arms of strangers again."

We were speechless. The illusion of good fortune had turned into a receding cloud of dust. Transfixed, Mother and I stared at each other, lost for words. Zeynab, on the other hand, was excited by her boldness, knowing she was treading on forbidden ground. "I shouldn't have said that," she moaned, tears welling up in her eyes. "You are such decent people. I bet you kick me out now. Right?" she asked, whimpering.

The phone rang and I lunged for it. A woman's voice I couldn't recognize asked for Zeynab. "Who are you?" I queried.

"I am her mother and have just arrived from Ghazvin."

"But madam," I said curtly, "she says her mother has died in a car crash."

"Oh, she's not all there, you know, and says things," the voice explained. "I'll be there to pick her up."

Mother, with her ear pressed against the receiver, wondered, apprehensively, "Who are these people? Where did they get our phone number and address?"

"They are after me," Zeynab said, "all those thieves and smugglers." If Auntie Malak had heard this, she would have fainted on the spot, I thought. Mother too looked pale, making me think that we were now in a real crisis.

"Do you know what you are talking about?" I snapped at Zeynab. "We have known Mohammad Agha for twenty years."

All this time, Zeynab kept glancing at me pleadingly, seemingly apprehensive of Mother and the misery that lay in her future. Words, as if churned by a force stronger than her will, poured out uncontrollably. Mother, vacillating and nervous, muttered, "Didn't I say we shouldn't hire anyone? Didn't I say we shouldn't trust anyone? How do we know what Mohammad Agha does in his spare time? He does only carpentry work here. We are not with him all the time. Who could have imagined Hassan Agha and that wife of his leaving us in a lurch after fifty years? Do you remember how she put her hand on her hips and stood in my face yelling, 'Then what's the revolution is for?'"

This was a delicate subject and had to be changed. I turned to Zeynab and asked if she could honestly tell us who she is and how she got to know Mohammad Agha. We all drifted into the kitchen, which looked meticulously clean after Zeynab had finished with it. Impressed, once more Mother changed her tone. "Listen to me, girl," she addressed Zeynab, "don't be afraid and tell me the truth. I won't let anybody hurt you—provided you tell me the truth."

"I swear on the Holy Koran, I'm telling the truth." Zeynab asserted. "Until a few years ago," she went on, "I was in an orphanage. Then I was adopted by a rich engineer, Mr. Shams-Akhtar, and his wife. Three years ago she died. Mr. Shams-Akhtar married me off and moved lock, stock, and barrel to America. Turns out my husband was a heroine-smuggling gang leader, him and his mother and brothers. They tried to get me hooked too, but I ran away and went to the Committee and gave them their names. The guards came and took them all away. A little later, I saw their pictures in the paper, and the report said that they'd hanged my husband and two of his brothers. That made me happy. Then this woman who says she's raised me took me to her house and that's where I saw Mohammad Agha. His job was to bring in girls. One night they sent a customer to my room, and I got into a fight with him. I cracked his skull with a flowerpot and ran into the street yelling and screaming. Mohammad Agha caught up with me and told me he would find me a job if I shut up about the whole thing. He was so afraid the Committee would find out. That's how I ended up here. And now you are going to kick me out, I know."

I was in a real quandary. Was she sincere? I could not tell. I wanted so desperately to see through her. I pulled Mother to the side. "We absolutely must protect her," I whispered, "if she is honest. We must change her life."

"Are you crazy?" Mother retorted. "It's dangerous. Didn't you hear? Heroin smugglers! She's sent her husband to the gallows. His comrades are not going to let go. They'll be after us. What if she'd tell the Committee all sorts of lies about us? I shouldn't have trusted Mohammad Agha. I never liked him that much. Come to think of it, he does look like a cutthroat. That stupid and bad-tempered Hassan Agha! He was worth his weight in gold, compared to these folks. Fifty hears he lived with us under one roof and not a pin got lost or misplaced, though he had control of everything in this house. What do we do now?" Mother said with a note of desperation in her voice. "I'm gonna call Mohammad Agha to come and get this girl out of here."

I felt it contingent upon me to show some backbone. "No way!" I ejaculated. "First we must get to the bottom of what she says. If she is telling the truth, we can't hand her over to those wolves."

Mother was reluctant. "What if she is in cahoots with those thieves?" she said, now in the throes of doubt. Trying to defuse the tension, I told her jokingly she was worse than Auntie Malak. It suddenly occurred to Mother that Zeynab had taken a shower in the downstairs bathroom and had possibly seen the crates of wine bottles left with us by a friend for safekeeping. "Those crates are behind the bathroom window in the backyard," she said fearfully. "I am sure she has seen them! Now she has an advantage over us. One word and she'll report us to the Committee. Imagine that! Here we are, our maid's captive!"

"We'd better not talk about the crates," I said dismissively. "I'll dispose of them tonight somehow."

"Throw them in an empty lot or something," she suggested. "To hell with that wine. I told you not to store them in the house."

Zeynab, oblivious to us, was mumbling to herself absent-mindedly and incoherently. "I had a good time in the engineer's house," she said to no one in particular. "Until his wife died and he went crazy. He'd cry every night and beat his head against doors and walls and then turn on me and give me a good thrashing." She then reached for an apple and started gnawing at it, quiet and pensive.

That night we had an invitation to dinner at Mr. K's home, and this added to our ordeal. We were torn between suspicion and sympathy. For a moment, allowing sentiment to take over, Mother said, "Poor girl, snatched up by these wolves! We can rescue her. I'll keep her here . . . find her a husband . . ." she muttered, her voice trailing off.

Before anything else, we had to do something about the wine crates, regardless of what we did with Zeynab. By now, we had thrown away all unsanctioned objects such as playing cards, backgammon boards, videos, music tapes, incriminating photos, etc., all in fear of a raid. Mother covered her head even when she answered the phone. We kept the windows shuttered, went to bed early, and turned off all lights. We had cut down on socializing—which had taken a toll on Mother's temper. She was already demoralized by Hassan Agha's departure and Morteza's grievance lodged with the authorities. After a couple of short visits to Europe, Mother had toyed with the idea of liquidating everything and moving to the other corner of the world to get away from all this. But she had decided against it. How would it possible to go into exile at her age to a land where streets evoked no memories and language was a barrier? How could one sit next to a small window all day and watch the never-ending European rain? Despite everything—the murderous Afghani wetbacks, religious-police raids, runaway inflation, Hassan Agha's desertion, war, bombardment, and insecurity—Tehran was home, and every part of it interlaced with her life. Even its problems and heartbreaks were meaningful and could be shared widely. Its rare moments of relief, too, were of a public nature. Death itself had familiar rituals, and life in this town, with all its chaos and agony, had familiar and comforting patterns for Mother and was latent with the expectation of better things to come. Living abroad, however, would have meant nostalgia for the past and recycling old memories.

Time was now of the essence and we had to take some action. Mother had the urge to do something drastic, something untoward, to protect

Zeynab, this helpless creature, but was scared of the consequences. She was more inherently cautious than to act on impulse. That made her so much more desperate for a reasonable escape route.

"Did you notice how casually she spoke of her husband's execution?" noted Mother. "She almost sounded jolly. It made my blood curdle. I don't even know these people. But when I see their pictures in the paper and read the caption they have been executed I get sick. But this girls sounds as if she is used to such things. She could do the same thing with us." At this point it looked like we had to get rid of her. But how? And how to deal with Mohammad Agha?

"I know you don't want me," said Zeynab, as if reading our thoughts instinctively. "I should have kept my trap shut. I know it was stupid of me to talk. I'm not going back to Mohammad Agha and that bitchy aunt of his. I just got myself out of their clutches. I know where I'll go."

"Where?" asked Mother expectantly.

"Back to the engineer, Mr. Shams-Akhtar," replied Zeynab with alacrity.

"But you said his wife is dead and he is in Europe," exclaimed Mother, thinking she had caught her at a lie. But Zeynab was right on the ball and came back with an answer. "But his mother is here and she liked me. Besides, I heard that he is now back," she came back without missing a beat.

The dry and hollow timber of Zeynab's voice told me that she was lying. But to Mother this was a ray of hope. "That's my girl," she whooped. "You just do that. If they kept you all those years, they must be better than anyone else. You just go to their house, and I'll put Mohammad Agha and his aunt in their place for good."

"But you don't know that woman," warned Zeynab. "A few months ago she had some problem with a neighbor, and she told a bunch of lies to the Committee. They came and took that woman away."

Once more the color drained out of Mother's face. She immediately regretted pitching herself against the aunt. "Very well," she said, in retraction of her threat, "I won't get tangled up with that woman. That is none of my business. As for you, dear girl, just go Mr. Akhtar's and stay there."

It was hard for her to utter these words but they had to be said. We had to extricate ourselves from Zeynab and her predicament. After all that had happened, we had to act conservatively and with self-preservation in mind.

As for the dinner party, it was decided that Zeynab should go with us. Mother helped her put on one of her old-fashioned winter garments with a high collar. When Zeynab saw herself in the mirror, she burst out laughing, almost like a child.

"I look just like the aunt, one of those madams," she said as she guffawed.

Mother winced. "Now you look respectable," she said defensively. "What was it you were wearing before? It was shameful."

While Zeynab was busy adjusting her outfit, I called a friend about moving the crates of wine. I knew Mr. K would take exception to having a stranger in his house, but we had no choice. We even thought of declining the invitation. But then we felt we needed the company. Besides, the affair was a farewell party for me in anticipation of my upcoming trip out of the country.

Mr. K did not easily let anybody in his house. He had made elaborate arrangements with trusted friends and relatives for coded ringing of the doorbell. He would alert his dogs to stand guard before he opened the door. The dogs had been especially trained to be suspicious of the chador and attack women wearing it.

When we arrived, we touched the door and a light came on at the top of the doorway. When we rang the doorbell, we could hear a siren sounding inside the house, setting off the dogs. A metallic voice in the intercom asked, "Who are you?" Then another voice from behind the door asked the same question for confirmation. Following a long pause, the door opened and we entered. We hastily took off the chadors and other headgear before the dogs reached us. Mr. K immediately stared at Zeynab, who was putting away her chador. He then looked quizzically at Mother. I intervened and explained that she was not a stranger but a new maid we could not leave at home because we didn't trust her that much. I hastened to point out that we were letting her go the next day any way. This not only failed to calm Mr. K, but exacerbated his agitation to such an extent that I began to regret coming to the party at all. Earlier that morning, sixteen people had been executed for an assortment of charges including corrupt practices and infractions of religious moral standards. This had put everyone on edge.

Mr. K asked us to wait out in the garden until he had warned his family and guests of the presence of a stranger in the house. Zeynab was certainly proving a disruptive factor among us. We were all related, close-knit and like-minded. That night a foreign element had infiltrated our gathering, causing concern and discomfiture. Mr. K's wife, adjusting her headgear, sidled up to Mother, wanting to know why she had trusted a stranger. Bringing Zeynab had definitely been a mistake, but it was too late.

Zeynab, oblivious to the disturbance her presence had caused, was delighted to be at an affair of that kind. With wide-eyed curiosity, she was looking everyone over. At some distance from where the guests had congregated, a chair was placed for her with a bowl of fruit and confectionaries at her feet. Soon it was time to tune in the Persian broad-cast from Radio Israel. My Uncle Doc was addicted to foreign broad-casts and knew the wave lengths and schedules of all of them. But Mr. K cast a wary glance at Zeynab and signaled to him not to turn on the radio.

Auntie Malak wanted to know what Zeynab's wages were. I noticed that Mother was not averse to the idea of palming Zeynab off on Auntie. Accordingly, she began giving a praising account of Zeynab's housekeeping virtues. She hinted that the girl needed a home and did not expect any pay. The only reason why we were trying to place her was that we were leaving town for an extended period. The thought of an unpaid domestic excited Auntie, but she was too nervous about strangers to fall for it.

The party was not like always. Mr. K, given to telling tired old jokes, was now silent. Auntie Malak, who loved to discuss the news and current affairs, was wordless and pensive. So was my uncle, who had been told not to turn on the radio. The younger folks, usually garrulous and strident, were quiet and sullen. Tooba Khanum's husband, always critical and ranting about the sorry state of affairs, seemed on the verge of an explosion, now that Mr. K had whispered in his ear, pointing to Zeynab, to keep his mouth shut.

At one point, when Zeyanb got up to go to the bathroom, the whole company simultaneously converged on Mother with questions. She held up her hand. "Listen," she almost yelled. "The girl is Mohammad Agha's niece, for goodness sakes. And you all know *him*. She is no stranger!"

Except for Mr. K, this was enough to set everyone's mind at ease. Even my uncle turned his radio on almost immediately. But Mother, always inclined to melodrama and wanting to share her anxieties with as wide an audience as possible, could not resist mentioning her uncertainties about Mohammad Agha's character. God only knows, she went on, but Zeynab had mentioned something about his involvement with heroine smuggling gangs. She then dropped the bombshell: Zeynab had informed on her husband, resulting in his execution by the authorities. At this point Auntie Malak gave a loud squeal, raising her hand to her throat. "Afghani, she is an Afghani, I knew it," she croaked through choking sounds. "I'm outa here," she said, turning to Mother, "So you wanted to pass this one on to me! How could you? Did you want to have me murdered? You can't trust anyone anymore, not even your own relatives!"

Mother appeared puzzled and looked at others questioningly. Mr. K, in extreme distress, looked at Mother and babbled, "These things are dangerous! Your son has just been released from prison. Just the mention of the word "opium" these days is enough to send you to the gallows."

"We shouldn't have brought the girl," said Mother somberly. "Let's go."

Now that the party was in disarray, no one objected to our departure. We called Zeynab, who was playing with some children in the hall and watching television, looking so harmless and vulnerable. I wanted so badly to believe that she was sincere and that I should take her under my wing against the dictates of common sense. But that was beyond me; I did not have the will power. When we got home, Zeynab was still in a buzz from the party and said nothing about leaving. She jumped in the bed she had spread in the downstairs hall and was asleep within minutes.

We had a rough night. In a state of high nervousness, Mother jumped at every sound. Early in the morning we were startled when the telephone rang. It was Zeynab's so-called aunt calling to talk to her. Mother spoke to her, calm and collected, explaining that we could not keep Zeynab because we were leaving for Europe. Sensing something was amiss, the aunt spoke diffidently. "I'm embarrassed," she said. "I should have told you the truth. This girl is a bit on the crazy side. Her father died some years ago, and her mother, my younger sister, lives in Ghazvin and is a mental patient. I have raised this girls and I know she takes after her mother. She comes up with strange tales. Her mother arrived in Tehran yesterday and is dying to see her. I apologize for inconveniencing you. I'll just come and get her."

"Not so fast," replied Mother. "Let me talk to her first to see what she says." Mother did not wait for a reply and hung up.

The aunt had sounded reasonable and credible enough for Mother to change her mind once more. " We shouldn't have judged Mohammad Agha so fast," she said thoughtfully. "He's worked for us twenty years and has always been sensible and level-headed. This girl is lying in her teeth, confusing us in the middle of all this chaos. Of course we can't keep her if she is a mental case."

Zeynab, who had been eavesdropping behind the door, burst into the room. "I am not waiting for Mohammad Agha and his gang to come and get me. I'm leaving right now," she said in a rage.

"Where are you gonna go? Back to the engineer?" I asked. "What engineer?" she spat back. She then looked at me morosely, as if she was going to continue, but the fluttering of a moth behind the windowpane caught her attention. She remained motionless for a moment before she came to herself and hurriedly put on her shoes and chador. Before we had time to react, she left the house, slamming the door behind her.

"Oh, my god, what do we tell Mohammad Agha?" said Mother, whimpering. "She was kind of entrusted to us."

For a while after Zeynab's departure, we were chafed with pangs of conscience. But soon a sense of relief came over us, now that the interlude was seemingly over. We were no longer involved. It was out of our hands. "Some people never change," said Mother, more in justification of our course of action than as a casual observation. "We tried to be charitable and give her a helping hand and look what a commotion she caused! Good riddance! Never mind that we don't have any household help any more." On this note we indulged in a moment or two of self-pity laced with an appropriate amount of sympathy for Zeynab and her kind, before putting the bizarre affair out of our minds and getting back to our normal routine.

Then came the first phone call of the day. It was Auntie Malak expressing her chagrin and disapprobation about our role in the events of the night before. For our part, we called Mr. K to tell him that the affair was over and he could relax. The doorbell rang just as we sat down for lunch. "It's Mohammad Agha," said Mother, considerably alarmed. She wanted me to answer the door and advised me that I deal with him firmly. I had no stomach for the encounter and felt a tinge of embarrassment.

Gingerly, I opened the door and was astonished by what I saw. There she was, Zeynab, perched on a motorcycle behind a dour-looking young man with a full, dark beard. Apparently delighted to see me, she jumped off the bike and rushed to the door. The young man averted his glance and stared at the ground, hinting that my head was not covered. "Excuse me a minute," I said, running back into the house to get my headgear. Mother followed me back to the door, panting, "Is she back? Has she blabbered to the Committee? What trouble are we in now?"

When Mother appeared at the door, the young man greeted her respectfully. "Dear lady," he said, "this girl is a distant relative of ours. Her father was a close associate of mine, God rest his soul, and we have known her family for a long time."

"According to her, though," replied Mother, somewhat sarcastically, "she's all alone in this world. We've been told a hundred different versions. How come she's found family and friends now?" The young man ignored the remark and proceeded to produce an identity card, which he held in front of Mother's face. "I am an employee of Ghods Department Store and this is my ID," he said assertively. "This young lady is my brother's fiancée. My brother was in the war front and took a shrapnel in the back, which paralyzed him. We ask that you look after her for a while until we know what's going to happen to my brother. It is not right that you let her roam the streets."

Zeynab furtively whispered in my ear, "He is lying. He is from the Committee."

We were in a terrible bind now. If that was true, we had no choice but to do his bidding. Before he roared off on his bike, he told us emphatically that we were not to turn her over to anyone else. We would be responsible if something happened to her.

Back to square one, we thought. Zeynab was elated, like a dog reunited with its owner. She threw off her chador and hung around my neck, kissing me on the cheek repeatedly. She then picked up the broom and started cleaning feverishly. "A ball of fire she is!" exclaimed Mother, unable to contain her delight with Zeynab's work. "I only wish she weren't off her rocker. Now that she has reported us to the Committee, we have no choice but to keep her for the time being."

Auntie Malak was coming to lunch, and we were at a loss what to tell her. A word about the Committee and she would have a heart attack. Mr. K would certainly sever relations with us altogether. So we called Auntie and postponed the lunch to another day, making some excuse. Meanwhile, Zeynab continued the work, humming under her breath and occasionally stopping to chuckle for no reason at all. When she finished, she announced that she wanted to take a shower. This triggered the anxiety over the wine crates in the backyard. I went hurtling down the stairs to see if they had been taken away—and they weren't. Frustrated, I ran upstairs and told Zeynab to hold off on the shower. I signaled Mother to keep an eye on her while I hid the crates in the utility room. "What the hell," said Mother impatiently. "Dump that filth down the toilet and throw away the bottles in an empty lot."

The wine did not belong to us but it was proving to be a serious liability to keep in the house. As Zeynab started on her lunch, I emptied the wine, stuffed the bottles in a sack, and threw them in the trunk of the car. I drove all the way to Gharb Township where friends of ours were having construction done, and flung the sack in a deserted corner of the lot. When I got back, Zeynab had finished lunch and was stretched out on her mattress fast asleep. There was a glow on her face, making her look sated, safe, and cheery. And I felt depressed. I was developing an affection for her, and that made me feel conflicted and at odds with myself. Every time she prevaricated or made up a new cock-and-bull story, she looked more pretty and likeable, eyes glinting and cheeks blushing, as if the risk of being caught at a lie added to her attractiveness.

The doorbell rang. It was Mohammad Agha. He walked in quietly, looking somber and demure. He was his usual self—noble and dignified, inspiring trust. What a monster had we made of him for ourselves! It was Zeynab who had ensnared us in her web of insane lies.

Deferentially, Mother invited him to take a seat and offered him tea. I turned to Zeynab and said that she should get packed and go with him. She grabbed my arm and drew me away, as she whimpered, eyes streaming, "I swear on the Koran, I swear to God, this man is worse than Shemr.[4] He has ruined hundreds of girls. Believe me, if you go to his aunt's house, you'd see what I mean. If you force me to go with him, how will you answer to God? Or the Committee?"

As I went over to talk to Mother privately, Zeynab's eyes followed me intently and she stared at us as we conferred. Her face was in a constant state of flux, like undulating forms on the surface of water, making it hard to fathom what lay beneath them. Her expression reflected fear and hope, sincerity and mischief. She looked so pitiful, and I felt simultaneously drawn to her and repulsed by her. Something enigmatic and mysterious pulsated from her that bewitched and frightened me at the same time—like dark unchartered terrain, full of promise and temptation but impenetrable and menacing, a disturbing dream unbound by the norms of reason and convention.

Once again, Zeynab looked guileless and vulnerable, moving in my direction to seek aid and solace. With eyes brimming with tears, in a voice soft and plaintive she whispered, "In the shower I was talking to God. I am not kidding. I don't say my prayers because I don't know the words, but I talk to God. When Mohammad Agha brought me here, I thought I was going to heaven. Your mother was an angel. So were you. I was crying in the shower, telling God they are good people; I must tell them the truth. Mohammad Agha had told me not to open my mouth, or I'd be kicked out. But something made me talk. I couldn't lie to you folks."

I was moved to certainty. She was telling the truth. Even if she wasn't, I had an overwhelming urge to believe her. I wanted her and her words to lower my defenses and overcome my resistance.

"This girl is crazy and a pathological liar. She has no idea who she is and where she comes from," Mother had determined.

Perhaps, I thought. But who were we, I asked myself, with all the genealogical charts and documented vital dates, well-defined thoughts, carefully assessed plans, clearly demarcated philosophical grounds, trivial pursuits, and major apprehensions, who were we?

"Zeynab will stay with us," I rumbled across the room. "We will not turn her over to anyone." Mother was so shocked by my announcement she could have been knocked down by a feather. But before she could raise her voice, I repeated the verdict. My heart palpitated with an undefinable exhilaration.

Wordlessly, Mohammad Agha finished the tea and stood up. He mumbled something by way of leave-taking and departed. As soon as the door closed behind him, Zeynab gave a shrill yelp and began laughing, laughing spasmodically and endlessly. I could not tell if she was laughing with joy or at having made a dupe out of me. It did not matter. I had done my deed and was happy about it. I had an urge to make her sit down and tell me her stories. I could also tell her the stories I had buried deep inside of me. Perhaps Mother's plan of marrying her off to a decent man who could be put to work for my brother and sending their offspring abroad for education, etc., etc., etc., could now be implemented.

We sat down to lunch in an eerie silence. We were all deep in thought, as if trying to make sense of the events of the past few days. None of us felt at ease.

Around four in the afternoon, Zeynab awoke from a nap and sat upright. "I had a terrible dream," she announced cheerlessly, but did not elaborate.

Around sunset, a telephone call came from the young man, the employee of Ghods Department Store. He wanted to talk to Zeynab. Mother, like someone suddenly awakened from a sleep, was dazed and confused. She stared at me quizzically. From the outside there were sounds of shouting and sporadic gunfire. I felt the onset of an anxiety attack and tried to collect my thoughts. Mother hurriedly drew the curtains tight shut and locked the front door, her face contorted with worry. Zeynab took the receiver and listened without saying a word. She seemed wan, and a bitter, defiant look came over her face. Her eyes lost that child-like impetuosity, looking more like those of a mature woman crushed under the weight of experience. She handed the receiver to my mother and said blankly: "I am leaving."

As she went to fetch her bag, the man explained to my mother that his brother had decided to marry Zeynab. Their mother, a pious woman, he remarked, would like to keep her for a while. He added that, God willing, we would be invited to the wedding.

"Wonderful, congratulations," intoned Mother reflexively. "Every young girl must marry someday."

"Easy for you to say," said Zeynab, almost disgustedly.

"Listen," I told her urgently. "You don't have to go if you don't want to. Wait, my brother knows the committee chief."

"What committee?" she said sneeringly.

"So," I spat out, hurt and angry, "all that talk of a marriage and the department store employee is another one your fabrications, huh?"

"What difference does it make?" she replied coldly, as she moved toward the door. "Unlucky folks are unlucky wherever they go."

At the front door, she turned and gazed in my direction. "In my dream this afternoon," she said, "I was in heaven, when a hand reached out and grabbed my hair and said I didn't belong there. I belonged in hell. I knew right there and then that I had to go."

I wanted so badly to stop her. I wanted for once to do something from the heart, something fantastic and irrational, but was immobilized with indecision, not able to find the courage to act.

"What do you think," asked Mother. "Was she telling the truth?"

---

[1] These so-called committees were created in the course of the revolution to orchestrate demonstrations in urban neighborhoods against the former regime. Later, they were unofficially in charge of enforcing civil laws and Islamic standards of social conduct.

[2] Proscribed Islamic covering for women in Iran.

[3] An agricultural region in central Iran.

[4] A detested villain in the tragedy of Karbala, the Shi'ite version of the defeat and eventual decapitation of Hussein, the fourth imam in the Shi'ite hagiography and the Prophet's grandson, at the hands of his political opponents.

A Mansion in the Sky

It was a rough summer. Intense heat. No water, no electricity. It was war, fear, and darkness. Massoud D, as if in the depths of a bad dream, confused, dazed and disoriented, dragged his wife and children all the way to Europe, without thinking, without knowing what lay ahead of him. Deliberately, he shunned common sense, caution, and circumspection. He showed no inclination to consult others more experienced than he, or more likely to stand their ground either because of fear of change and displacement or of some kind of a moral precept based on the love of one's homeland and belief in its cultural heritage.

Massoud hated the war and feared annihilation. He was sick and tired of incessant anxiety attacks. He had a senseless urge to get away and settle somewhere safe and secure, far away from all the commotion, bombs, explosions, and the possibility of dying or going insane. He made the arrangements with the speed of summer lightening. The household goods were auctioned off, and the house was sold to the first bidder, way below market value. Visas were obtained, tickets bought, suitcases packed. And then, just before departure, he caught sight of his old mother and proceeded to fall apart. "What will happen to her?" he asked himself. He felt an excruciating pain in the pit of his stomach as his entrails twisted and turned at the thought. Momentarily, he forgot his fear of death and destruction and delayed his decision to leave.

His mother, Maheen Banou, had watched, silently and without protest, all the time that the sale of the household was going on. She had seen strangers roam through the house and had not said a word. She had squatted in a corner against a wall, passing her hand over the Tabrizi rug, an heirloom, and tracing its floral designs and golden patterns with her fingertips. It was the relic of bygone days, the remnant of old, familiar things. It felt warm, but like a body in the final moments of life. She had clawed at the tassels of a tablecloth in an attempt to save it from disappearing. Her gaze had followed the china bowls as they were passed from hand to hand by prospective buyers. The tall Russian floor lamps, too, had been sold. Several time she had the urge to yell, "No! Not my sequined wrappers and betrothal mirror!" She had even thought of hiding some of the treasured items for keepsakes. Instead she had kept her silence, sitting quietly and unobtrusively in a corner, bleeding emotionally from inner wounds. She had watched the wall clock, the china plates, and the gilded picture frames disappear one after another. As she let them go, she had felt the despondency of a mother watching her children one by one abandoning her in favor of faraway places. She knew that hard times were ahead. But she had accepted her fate with no resentment against her son. Years ago she had deeded the house over to him with the proviso that it should not be sold while she lived. But this was an old agreement made in the old days, before the revolution, before the war, before the fear had set in and dispersed the family. Maheen Banou wished for nothing but the well-being and happiness of her son, or her daughter for that matter, who was married to an Englishman and lived abroad. She would give anything, including her life, to see them happy and content.

For their part, the children were dedicated to her. Massoud had no intention of abandoning her, homeless and destitute, to save his own skin. But, then, in the chaos and destruction of war, he had lost his bearings and was not responsible for his compulsiveness. Maheen Banou, in her maternal sensitivity, realized this. That was the reason why she had kept quiet and out of his way. But she had cried. She had cried bitterly and alone, in the dark privacy of her bed, behind the closed door of the bathroom and at the end of the garden behind the tall cedars. She was attached to the old tapestry and odds and ends left over from the happy days of her youth, bequeathed to her by her father and her husband, both now deceased. Over the years, she had developed a bond with them. The memories of her entire life floated throughout the old house, and every brick and stone bore the imprint of her childhood experiences. This was the only place she had known as home and now she did not own this "place." In fact, she did not own any place in the world any more. She was in a void, suspended in mid-air. She wished she could just walk away and, like a dying cat, disappear from sight. Yet, she felt very much alive and unwilling to die, as if her age had been imposed upon her by others who arbitrarily dismissed her as old. The image she had of herself was lodged in sweet memories of her youth, reflected in the old mirror of yesteryears. Her heart pounded steadily in her breast, and she looked forward to the coming of spring and summer, to a future with her relatives and offspring who, at last count, numbered upwards of seventy. The others figured her age in terms of her birth date or marriage. But, Maheen Banou did not feel a day older than forty. This was what she felt and believed. But now, what was she to do? She felt superfluous and like an extinguished star out of the celestial orbit, exiled to the chaotic desolation of unchartered space. She wished she did not exist. But death was distant from her, and she groped with her toes to feel the solidity of the earth. Her body avidly absorbed the particles of light and warmth, and her thoughts, with myriad invisible cords, tied her to the sweet nooks and crannies of her past life.

It was arranged for Maheen Banou to stay with her sister for a few weeks or more (as long as two or three months, perhaps) until Massoud had established himself in Paris, found an apartment and a job, and settled into a routine. And then, all in good time, conveniently and with ease of mind, he would send for her to join him. Her daughter also had been thinking about her. Despite the modest income and the high cost of living, she called frequently, inviting her to London. Her English husband, too, magnanimously insisted on hosting his mother-in-law. But everybody emphasized the need for patience. Eventually, everything would work out, perhaps better than before. And Maheen Banou was known for her resilience and wisdom. Her children always said that they owed her whatever they had by way of native intelligence.

The first two weeks in her sister's house was especially hard on Maheen Banou. She was not in the habit of moving from place to place. Displacement proved very difficult to get used to. She was attached to her own room and her own bed and pillows. She was used to the sounds that came from the alley and the noises that her old neighbors made. She was almost addicted to the cooking odors that wafted from the kitchen and the familiar spots of dampness on the wall along the staircase. And, of course, there was the fragrance from the honeysuckle vine at the foot of her window and the sight of the four aspens planted at the far end of the compound to mark the occasion of her father's birth.

Maheen Banou's sister was kind and hospitable. Her husband, Dr. Yunes Khan, was uncommunicative and withdrawn, acutely missing his own seven children who had all left the country after the revolution. His eldest son lived in Australia and was beyond reach. Two daughters (the Terrible Twins) were in the United States. The middle son was knocking about in the Far East somewhere in the region that included Singapore, Japan, and Thailand. The youngest son was moving around and had no clear address. One other girl (according to the old doctor's muddled recollection) was a resident of Canada, or India, or some little-known country in Africa.

Maheen Banou and her sister were close. This had given Massoud the assurance he needed to put his conscience at ease. His mother would be comfortable and happy with her sister. Actually, that was the case until her sister's husband, Dr. Yunes Khan, lost his nerve in the incessant rocket attacks and began to show signs of psychosis. He started to have stray thoughts and bouts of paranoia. He was observed eavesdropping on the members of the household and searching the handbags of his wife and sister-in-law. He would hide some of his personal effects and get flustered when he couldn't find them. He would complain to his wife that Maheen Banou had filched his cigarette lighter and sunglasses. His wife would strenuously object, and that would lead to bitter quarrels between them. Maheen Banou heard snatches of their squabbling and twitched with pangs of mortification. The situation deteriorated to the point that made Maheen Banou count the days until she could leave and join her children in Europe. At the same time, she felt sorry for the old physician and knew that he was not consciously unkind and malignant. She did not blame him when he intentionally crushed her finger in the door jamb, causing the nail to come off, or the time when in the middle of the night he burst into her room and ruffled her bed and searched her pockets, ostensibly looking for his agate ring. She never whimpered or complained. She assured herself that the situation was transitory. She was glad her children were in good health and she herself, despite everything, was still alive and in full possession of her senses.

The much-awaited day finally arrived. Still thinking she was in a dream, Maheen Banou arrived in Paris and was reunited with her son. With eyes streaming (although she was very reserved and inhibited in showing emotion in the presence of others), Maheen Banou showered her grandchildren with kisses and hugged them repeatedly. It was as if she had no intention of taking any rest, despite the tension and rigors of the flight from Tehran, which involved waiting in long lines and being searched by the customs inspectors. In the process, she had lost her medication pouch and misplaced her eyeglasses. She had also been further encumbered by aching feet and a sudden bout of vertigo. And of course there was the damned air-sickness as soon as she was airborne. Nevertheless, if they had let her, she would have gone on talking and fawning over her grandchildren and daughter-in-law all night as she moved around the tiny apartment and asked repetitive and confused questions.

But she was eventually persuaded to retire. They gave her the children's bedroom for the first couple of nights and bivouacked the children on the living-room floor. Discreetly, they had told the children that Grandma had just arrived and needed special consideration and that she'd be moved later and they could have their room back. The sour looks on the faces of the children and their disgruntled silence had not escaped Maheen Banou's notice. She felt a twinge and opened her mouth to say something, but could not find the nerve. Besides, she was exhausted and her whole body trembled with fatigue. She passed out before her head hit the pillow. But in the middle of the night she woke up with the sensation of a heavy weight pressing on her chest. She was needled by a curious mixture of humiliation and guilt circulating through her body like a physical pain. She could not forget the resentful look on the faces of her grandchildren. She was tormented by the thought of depriving them of their room. It was as if she lay on a bed of nails and wished she had slept in the corridor or squatted against a wall in some corner. On the third day, she was moved out of the children's room—which she welcomed with a sigh of relief—and assigned a corner of the living room floor where she could sleep on a foam mattress. In the morning, she would roll up the mattress and stow it away under a sofa. She kept her suitcase in the kitchen and dragged her handbag around wherever she went. All the closets in the apartment were bursting with clothes. Various household articles were stuffed under every bed, sofa, and chair. There was no room to move. Maheen Banou, who had spent her life in a spacious house with large sunny rooms, felt especially cramped and claustrophobic. After all, she was used to her old house that had vast closets and storage space, an attic large enough to hold a hundred suitcases, and a cellar that could accommodate a truckload of stuff. Well, she thought, that was all in the past, and life was full of ups and downs. Sleeping on the living-room floor, too, had a charm of its own. Of course, the noise from the street was bothersome, and the rumble of the underground trains rattled doors and windows. But, Maheen Banou had convinced herself that it was the way Europeans lived their lives and there was nothing she could do about it. Thank goodness she was with her family and her life was settled into a routine.

Her grandchildren too seemed happy with the way things had shaped up for them and seemed to get along well with a handful of Arab and Portuguese schoolmates. Sometimes the family entertained. On those occasions, Maheen Banou had to remove her bedding from the living room and look for another spot around the house. But where? The apartment had two bedrooms, one kitchen, and a tiny bathroom with a commode in a corner. She couldn't very well sleep in the couple's bedroom, although her son had insisted on it and her kindly daughter-in-law had registered no protest. The children's bedroom was too congested: two beds side-by-side and the floor cluttered with books, socks, shoes, tennis rackets, and a soccer ball. The only possibility was the kitchen. She would not mind. Not that she took up a lot of space—as diminutive, delicate, and brittle as she was. She could easily fit in a closet or under a bed. In fact, she had spent a couple of nights in the bathtub. Surprisingly, she had found it fairly comfortable and had been able to sleep. But her son had vehemently objected to the arrangement and had forced her to take his place next to his wife. That night had been one of the worst for Maheen Banou. She had not been able to sleep a wink. She was ill at ease lying next to her daughter-in-law. The sheets felt prickly, and her body glowed with the heat of embarrassment. She crawled to the edge of the bed and bundled herself into a fetal position so tightly that she was almost like a little ball that would fall off the bed with the slightest push and roll to the corner of the room. The young woman tolerated the situation for a few nights and then gently let her husband know that she would not stand for it. Massoud, usually mellow and level-headed, unaccountably exploded in his wife's face with such force that his voice could be heard all over the apartment, causing alarm and fear in the children. This was followed by an argument of unprecedented bitterness between them. As the couple shouted at each other, Maheen Banou died a thousand times. She cursed herself for having intruded in their lives and came to the resolution to leave that very minute. She packed her meager belongings in a suitcase, got dressed, and sat on a bench out in the corridor. She sat there trying to calm down and think rationally about her next move. Where was she to go? Back to Tehran, perhaps. That was the logical thing to do. Back to her sister's. But that meant having to endure the antics of Dr. Yusef Khan. No way, she thought. What about her cousin? Then, she remembered that the woman had died a couple of months before. The thought brought a lump to her throat. Possibly, she could stay with her paternal cousins or nephews. But, they had all emigrated to the U.S. Then, it would have to be the grave-yard or the bottom of hell. Even if she had to beg on the street or be a housemaid, she would be in her own country where she could lay her head down and die. One thing was certain: she would not stay here any more.

As luck would have it, a call came from her daughter in London that morning insisting that Maheen Banou be put on a plane immediately to come over and stay with her. It was a few days before the formalities were taken care of and Maheen Banou was driven to the airport for the flight to London. She had a sense of freedom like a bird just let out of the cage. The plane was like a house, warm and secure. She had the seat all to herself, and nobody could lay claim to it. She would be satisfied with just as much on the ground. When the meal was served, she ate it with appetite. The stewardess reminded her of her maid, Nana Khanum.

In the old days, Nana Khanum had served Maheen Banou her meals meticulously set on a tray. Maheen Banou was heart-broken and cried profusely when the news came that Nana Khanum's grandson had been killed in the war and her son had gone insane and had to be committed. If this had not happened, perhaps things would have been different. After all, Massoud had intended to lease a small house and relegate her to the care of Nana Khanum. This would have been the best solution for all concerned. But no one could predict the disaster. They soon learned that the boy's head had been blown off by a shrapnel. In time, relatives arrived from Sabzevar, Nana Khanum's hometown, and there was such a heart-rending scene. The emissaries came from the Committee and the Martyr Foundation bearing the official "condolences and felicitations" on the occasion of the young man's martyrdom. Subsequently, Nana Khanum was given a stipend and living quarters in Sabzevar, where she went to stay. All of this had happened before Maheen Banou moved in with her sister.

Maggie (formerly Manijeh) hugged Maheen Banou so hard that she gasped for air, feeling a mixture of pain and ecstasy in the tight squeeze of her daughter's arms. The son-in-law also gave her a warm embrace and a kiss. David Oakley was a nice man. He was of Jewish descent, hence his affectionate nature, Maheen Banou thought. She had always been uneasy about having a Jew for a son-in-law. She would have preferred an Iranian and a Muslim one. However, she never said anything to her daughter, as she did not like to interfere in the affairs of her children. But on that day, when she saw David's wholesome look and his friendly, sincere eyes, she felt relieved and comfortable. She leaned on David's manly arm and gave him an open smile. Standing next to him, Maheen Banou was even more aware of her own smallness. The top of her head did not even come up to David's waist. Weighing forty kilos or less, she felt light as a bird, with porous bones and spindly legs.

The day was rainy and a cold wind blew. David stored the suitcases in the trunk of his car and gave Maheen Banou's bony shoulder a jolly pat. In the car, Maggie sat next to her mother and lay her head on her aching shoulder whispering in her ear that she would never let her go back to Paris or Tehran. The tenderness of the moment made Maheen Banou's heart race with joy. She closed her eyes and drifted into a dreamless sleep.

The apartment was on the fourth floor. No elevators, though. Maheen Banou was too tired and groggy to negotiate the stairs. David Oakley swept her bodily off the ground, at which she gave a scream and stiffened herself like a rod. Maggie laughed heartily, and David, in a jovial and effusive mood, started climbing the stairs carrying Maheen Banou tucked under his arm, not unlike a wooden doll. Maheen Banou was completely immobilized and incredulous. She did not know whether she wanted to yell or cry. This was an entirely new sensation. She had absolutely no frame of reference from which to react to this situation. She felt she was not herself, that she had become an object, a broom, or a chair, which the couple had bought at a store. Being a broom was a new state of mind, a new dimension of her existence.

If anything, David and Maggie's apartment was even smaller than Massoud's in Paris; it had only one bedroom. They had no children, true, but they had a big, shaggy dog almost the size of Maheen Banou. David Oakley was a pragmatic man and conducted his affairs in accordance with the dictates of reason and good sense. He shunned sentimentality and never minced his words. Maheen Banou would sleep on the living room couch and stay out of the way in the bedroom when there was company. This was not a desirable arrangement, but the best of all possible solutions under the circumstances. Maheen Banou had no objections. In fact, she never had any objections. Even if she did, she would not voice them. This made life easier for everyone.

David Oakley was a lecturer in economics and kept a close watch on household expenses. As minuscule as her appetite was, Maheen Banou tried to eat even less to reduce the burden on the family budget. Maggie took accounting courses at the college. This meant that the couple left early in the morning and returned late in the evening, exhausted and brooding. If they had any conversation at all, it was about the high cost of living. Maheen Banou had no money of her own. But, upon arrival, she turned over her gold bracelet and ruby earrings to her daughter for liquidation. Maggie had been reluctant to accept them. "No," she had said. "It is impossible." But her husband had said, "No problem." Maggie had continued to demur and had even shed a few tears. But in the end, reluctantly and with her husband's strong urging, she had agreed to the sale.

It was here that Maheen Banou had got into the habit of talking to herself. She could not communicate with her son-in-law, and Maggie had to talk to her husband in English. Often, she chose not to say anything at all. The dinner was always a quiet affair after which Maggie got busy on her homework. David turned his attention to the newspaper, which he seemed to read from cover to cover, every word on every page. Afterwards, they turned on the television. They watched only cultural programs and talk shows. Maheen Banou stared at the screen uncomprehendingly and was soon adrift in the world of her own thoughts and recollections of other times and places. During the day, when she was home alone, she would clean and tidy up the apartment and tend the two flowerpots on the window ledge or simply watch the rain fall interminably from the gray sky. Sometimes, weather permitting, she would venture out and sit on a bench in the neighborhood park, shivering with cold. That winter was exceptionally harsh, and Maheen Banou caught a cold. First, there was some inflammation in her throat. Later, the cold affected her lungs, causing violent fits of coughing. She coughed so hard it felt like her entrails were dislodged. Worst, the next-door neighbor was disturbed by her coughing and occasionally banged on the wall in protest. Mortified, Maheen Banou shoved her head under the pillow or stuffed the bed sheet in her mouth to stifle the noise.

Things changed with the coming of the spring. Occasionally, a few rays of sunlight worked their way through the clouds and warmed hearts and bodies. David Oakley managed to get three days off to take his wife and mother-in-law for a spin in the country. They all had a good time. Maggie had brought along some medication and geriatric tonic, which helped Maheen Banou to put on two kilos. She was very grateful for all this and was starting to feel at home when there were new complications. With the arrival of the summer, time came for the couple to take their customary two-month vacation in the highlands of Scotland, staying with David's aunt. Obviously, Maheen Banou could not go. She could not stay in the apartment either because it had been subleased, as it always was, while the couple was away from London. This was a measure to augment the family income, and it was so much more understandable now that there was the added expense of keeping the mother-in-law. A decision was made, ad hoc, to pack Maheen Banou off to Paris for the duration. In fact, Maheen Banou was in the air before Massoud was called to let him know of her imminent arrival.

This was exceptionally bad timing for Massoud. Although he was always delighted to see his mother and had said that he would heartily welcome her at any time, at this particular moment he could not possibly accommodate her in his immediate plans. It was, after all, the summer vacation time, and the family was about to go to the south of France. There was, of course no money for hotels and waterfront villas. So they were planning to pitch tents on the beach or in the wilderness—in the forest for example—or campgrounds. In any case, there was no way for Maheen Banou to tag along. The brother and sister argued on the phone. David had a few suggestions, and, after lengthy consultations, it was decided that Maheen Banou should fly back to London where some kind of provision would be made for her stay.

Although the discussions were not supposed to be in Maheen Banou's earshot, she heard enough to wish the ground would split and swallow her up. She was tired of seeing herself being passed around like a cumbersome, undesirable object.

Maggie approached Firoozeh Khanum, one of her close friends, who eked out a modest living by running a small laundromat. She was a good-natured woman with a sense of humor. Her own living quarters, she explained, were simply too small to accommodate a guest. However, there was some storage space in the back of the shop, which had no windows but was warm and safe. David Oakley went for it. Maggie had qualms, but no choice. To bring the issue to a close, Maheen Banou agreed to be housed in the back of the shop.

The room was small, damp, and dark. Maheen Banou cried bitterly the first night she was there. She begged God to take her life. She wandered what it was that made her cling to life so tenaciously. She decided it was her love for her children. She wished it would leave her heart so she could die peacefully.

Kind and gentle, Firoozeh Khanum was more capable than ten men put together. She had a husband who still lived in Tehran. Evidently, he was one of those self-indulgent opium addicts who came to London once a year, at his wife's expense, only to rave and rant about the way he was being treated by the world. He was doleful, bloated, and ineffectual. In the past, he had been—rather, claimed to have been—somebody on the literary scene with a marginal reputation in writing and translating. But, with the first glimmer of hard times ahead, he had succumbed to depression and defeat. His wife, on the other hand, had no use for whining, moaning, and groaning. Early on, she had dispatched her children to England and followed them there to set up the laundromat in order to provide for them. She was by nature giving and magnanimous. She did her best to help those around her who deserved help. She took one look at Maheen Banou, at her sweet face and sad, hazel eyes, and decided that she liked her. She did her shopping for her and attended to her needs. During the day, she would set her up in the shop among the washing machines and bring Persian books and newspapers for her to read and entertain herself.

Soon, through the grapevine, Maheen Banou's brother, Karim Khan, heard about his sister's humiliating condition and was massively outraged. He lived in Canada in relative affluence on a farm where he raised birds and rabbits. He was so indignant that he wrote harsh letters to his nephew and niece and berated them for the selfish treatment they had accorded their mother. (Perhaps he was too harsh, he thought later, but he was moved beyond control.) He demanded that arrangements be made for Maheen Banou to move in with him. Through the auspices of a friend at the Canadian embassy, he obtained a visa for her and sent airline tickets for the trip. When Massoud and Maggie protested, he called them on the phone and yelled at them. Since he was the eldest member of the family, they withdrew their objections.

It was in early winter when Maheen Banou took off for Canada. The prospect of the flight, which was to be her longest, pleased her. On the plane, she was seated next to the window. She would stare at the bright translucence outside the plane for long periods. Her seat was warm and comfortable. That was all she wanted, a place all her own, immune from the encroachment by others. She had a slight fever, and the warmth of the sun felt good on her face. She would doze off for a while, her head dropping to her chest. Then she would slowly wake up and gaze, dreamily and heavy-lidded, at the vastness of the space that extended to the far horizon. Below her were fields of white fluffy clouds, bright, weightless, and pristine, as in a celestial reverie, in the insouciant dreams of the archangels.

The passenger in the adjoining seat whispered something to her that she did not understand. She declined the proffered tray of food and turned her face to the window. With her feverish eyes, she took in the sunlight streaming through the window. She felt as if countless little stars were scattered in her skull, twinkling in the maze of her confused thoughts. She had a curious sensation, as if a bright light was burning inside her. The blue of the sky was even and uninterrupted. No patches of clouds or air turbulence disturbed the vastness that stretched from the primeval moment to the last frontier of imagination, an expanse undefined by any shape or form, unmeasured by any scale. Against it, Maheen Banou saw herself when she was twelve or so years old playing on the grounds of the family estate at the foot of Mount Damavand. She could see the snow falling and the tips of her fingers getting numb from touching it. She would stare at the gray horizon through the rapidly falling snowflakes, and that would give her a momentary levitating sensation, as if her feet were off the ground and she was rising through the air. She loved to play this game. Even as an adult, she had indulged in it. On snowy days, she would place herself near the window in her room. Nana Khanum would bring her tea and lumps of hard candy. Like zombies, they both would stare at the blank whiteness outside and the drifting flakes of snow. After a while, sleep would set in. Waking up in the middle of the night, Maheen Banou would know that the snow was still falling and she would listen to the silence of the sleeping city, frozen under the cover of snow, like an uninhabited house with all the furnishings covered under clean white sheets. Nothing was audible except a magical stillness that permeated the space and overwhelmed the senses with the peaceful presence of a divine, ethereal being.

Through the long hours of the flight, Maheen Banou sat staring out of the window, feverish and perspiring but joyous and blissful. She had lost track of time and who or where she was. She would drift in and out of sleep, now dreaming, now awash in a sea of distant memories. She felt as if she was reeling in the air, through the dancing snowflakes, gliding, swinging. She was everywhere and in all ages of time; simultaneously, she saw a thousand likenesses of herself in different stages of her life, in infancy, youth, and old age—plastered all over the earth and sky. She saw herself and incarnations of herself in other lives. She was a woman multiplied infinitely, replicated in an endless series that wrapped round and round eternity. For the first time in her life, she had no awareness of her children, or, for that matter, of anyone else she knew on earth. All her earthly recollections, even those of her large Tabrizi-tapestry embroidered shawls and the Pahlavi Avenue house, had been obliterated.

High above the clouds, the vast expanse of the sky seeped into her being and settled in the depths of her soul. Like the soothing warmth of an Indian summer, damp and lascivious, it enclosed her in a cocoon and she felt safe and beyond the reach of time in the womb of the universe.

Impatiently, Karim Khan awaited the arrival of his sister. He had determined to keep her with him and had a vague sense of shame for what he thought was an uncaring attitude on the part of her children. The moment he laid eyes on Maheen Banou, he burst into tears, partly because he too felt isolated and homesick. Everyday he thought of returning home but had always managed to deter himself. Seeing his sister, old and dilapidated and homeless, gave rise to his longing for home. "To hell with this kind of life!" he muttered to himself. For a moment, he felt the compulsion to grab his sister and rush back to Tehran where he had a home and property, where the two of them could live together. As siblings, they had not had much age difference and had always been close.

Karim Khan was horrified by his sister's appearance when he saw her at close range. She looked emaciated, wan, and confused. She gazed at him but gave no sign of recognition. It was as if she was not in control of her senses. When Karim Khan held her hand, he was shocked. It felt like a hot piece of bone. He tried to talk to her, but she was dazed and unresponsive. Her answers were vague and indistinct. Distraught and concerned, Karim Khan embraced her sister and gave her a flurry of kisses. Touching her made him feel old, and a dart of pain shot through his heart.

As soon as they arrived home, Karim Khan made his sister comfortable in a large bed and called a doctor. Afterwards, he telephoned Maheen Banou's children and briefed them on her state of health. He tried to make light of the situation and attributed her condition to fatigue, sleeplessness, and high blood pressure. "It is not serious. No need to worry," he told them. He then turned to caring for his sister, joyously and enthusiastically. He had a lot to talk about and did not know where to begin. He talked of the past, of childhood days, yesterday, and the day before. He talked about himself and his impromptu decision to go back home. The idea exhilarated him. He could not believe that he had finally made the decision. He was not sure how he had found the courage, but he knew his sister had something to do with it. The vacuous expression on her face and her disorientation had given him a jolt. He looked into her blank eyes, drained of all familiarity and rational thought, and was beset by a vague fear. He saw her as an embodiment of banishment. This made him tremble with dismay. Through her, he had a realization of his own isolation and loneliness. He saw himself uprooted and adrift like a lonely passenger, a transient in a cold and dreary railway station. He held Maheen Banou's hand and kissed it. "This is the end of our wandering," he whispered into her uncomprehending ear. They would go home after she got well. Maheen Banou closed her eyes and, against her eyelids, saw herself in an airplane seated next to the window. She heard the blue expanse of the sky calling her. In her sleep, she saw the sky in a state of flux as a body of water, its waves lapping at the shores of light.

She had no idea how long she had been asleep, but a parched feeling in her throat woke her up. She raised up on shaky legs. Karim Khan was not in the house. She looked around the strange, unfamiliar room, not knowing where she was. A soft ray of light streamed in through the sheers hanging at the window. She walked toward it but had to hold the back of a chair, gasping with exhaustion. Then she took two more steps toward the window, but the effort proved monumental, bringing beads of sweat to her brow. With a tremulous hand, she moved the drapes aside and looked at the snowy day outside. She strained to hear the sound of cascading snow, the same inviting sound of silence she was used to hearing when it snowed heavily. She had a curious awareness of a presence in the room. She swung around and near the door saw the figure of Nana Khanum carrying tea and candy on a tray. She was sobbing. Of course, she had lost her grandson. "Wait," Maheen Banou heard herself say, "I have some money for your trip." She reached for the door handle and leaned on it, subdued and fatigued. She had a powerful urge to squat, but she had to find her seat on the plane. The stewardess was checking the ticket. A blast of cold air made her shiver. Snow was coming down in large, saucer-size flakes. She took another step and slipped. It was cold inside the plane, and she had yet not found her seat. She started walking down a white path ahead, but the snow was blinding. From a distance, Mount Damavand glared down. It was tall and majestic, like her father when he stood in prayer, with the wind twirling his mantle about him. It appeared as if his head scraped the sky and his feet had driven roots into the earth. The days in her life when she lived at the foot of Mount Damavand with its magical, formidable height had been the best of times, the days when her father stood in plain daylight on the stoop of the summer house, flanked by marble pillars, casting a shadow to the end of time. It was such a joy to crawl under his mantle and climb onto his shoulders. It was the highest spot in the world from which the buildings looked humble and people ant-like and insignificant. That was the way things looked from the window of the plane. It was as if she was perched atop her father's shoulders once again, beyond the reach of everyone: her mother, who admonished her; the dour religious teacher who vexed her with the talk of sin and repentance; the neighborhood constable who had once pulled her ear. Not even her husband, who set the limits of her liberty, could touch her. She was even safe from her children who clung unto her and devoured her flesh and blood with animal ferocity. Nor was she within the reach of those who set moral standards and historical precedents for her, those who measured her intellect and surveyed the periphery of her thought with the short ruler of geometry and the dismal measures of mathematics.

Someone was calling her name, as if from behind Mount Damavand. She broke into a run around the foot of the mountain, and an avenue opened up to her left, packed with fresh snow. Now she felt burning hot. She slipped out of her frock and unbuttoned her dress. Then she held her face up to the sky and remembered the little game of her childhood. She chuckled and a snowflake lit on her lip and it tasted sweet. She stared and stared, unblinking, at the descending snowflakes. Gradually, she felt her feet leave the ground as the flakes hung suspended in mid air. She rose into the sky, above the clouds, above Mount Damavand. On its peak, there was a huge armchair made of walnut, upholstered in red velvet—like the one in her father's study—to which the airline stewardess ushered her. Her special, reserved seat! When she sat down, she felt small like a child, dwarfed by the dimensions of the chair. She wrapped her father's mantle around her and leaned her face against the window. The sky was an even blue, radiating light and space, expansive and generous. She felt its gaze upon her. As she listened intently, she could only hear the muffled sound of falling snow and the welcome silence of death.

There were recriminations. Massoud D blamed his sister who, in turn, complained about her uncle Karim's heavy-handedness. David Oakley mused on the frequency of such phenomena. Since he was a university professor, he explored the relationship between cause and effect and such factors as historical and economic imperatives. Firoozeh Khanum felt genuine grief but got over it. Others tried to keep fresh in their minds Maheen Banou's fate but failed. What with all the hardships of making a living, the fatigue, the problems of a stalemated war, and coping with life in exile, how could one be expected to maintain such memories and recollection in the forefront of one's consciousness? Maheen Banou would have understood. Thank goodness she was so reasonable and understanding.

The Bizarre Comportment of Mr. Alpha in Exile

It was early in the morning when Mr. Alpha woke up, agitated and with a heavy heart. He felt uncomfortably frigid, and a dull anxiety circulated in his body like a physical pain. He listened intently and could hear someone walking on the upper floor. In the adjoining apartment, he heard the rush of water in the bathroom, and a church bell tolled morosely in the distance. He was reluctant to wake up, even to think. The day breathed heavily behind his closed eyelids and he was unwilling to face it. The daylight would reveal things with a starkness that made him uneasy. He rolled around in bed and pulled the bed sheets over his face, and in the darkness behind his closed eyes, watched the last dregs of sleep disappear in the wake of his half-awakened consciousness. He dozed off momentarily and in the short span of that sleep had a long dream. He dreamed of people he had never known and cities he had never seen and was brought back to a dazed wakefulness by the racing of his heart. As if in the grip of a massive hallucination, he stared at the strange objects and shadows around him. In the corners of the room lurked a hollow and unfamiliar smell that evoked no memories in his mind. He heard a key turn in a lock somewhere and the rumbling of a passing train. The rain beat intermittently on his windowpane. Perhaps it was early in the evening, or late in the morning, or before dawn. He stretched out his legs, retracted them, and turned over his stomach, letting his arm dangle by the side of his bed. His fingers, as if groping for a friendly or familiar touch, felt the cold wooden floor and the base of a damp wall where the aging wallpaper had peeled off. "Where am I?" he wondered in his groggy mind and immediately came to a full realization of his strange surroundings. He sat upright in bed for a second and then turned on the bedside lamp. He was now fully awake. There he was, the same Mr. Alpha, fifty-two, Iranian, Muslim, former teacher of history at Shapoor High School, until recently of Tehran. And now he was here, in a dingy sunless room at the end of the corridor on the fifth floor of a tenement in the Twentieth Prefecture, Paris.

"How lucky you are!" Mrs. Nabovat had written to him in a recent letter. "I wish we could be there, too, in that Garden of Eden, that crowning glory of all cities of the world!" The letter was stained, with teardrops most likely, which had made the ink run in places. She had pressed the back of each page against her red-painted lips and had left the impression of a kiss. "How very good for you to be there!" she had repeated at the end of her letter. "I wish I could be there with you." Uncannily, the letter conjured up a strong sense of her presence. It was sweet, it was verbose, and it gave off the aroma of fresh spices and home-cooked meals. His mother's letter, on the other hand, was drenched with complaints about aching feet and worsening glaucoma. She had written of her misgivings of blindness and fears of dying in desolate destitution. The letter was imbued with the finality of her last will and testament. As if she had no hope of ever seeing her son again, she had solemnly exhorted him to be diligent in that land of infidels in the maintenance of his health and preservation of his faith and virtue—and his money.

His uncle's letter was equally depressing. Business was stagnant and his debts were mounting. His sons had gone into hiding, and he was constantly irked by nagging neighbors and revolution-crazed customers. "My dear nephew," he had written in his characteristically stilted style. "We at long last had to sell the Tabrizi carpet and with it went our last hedge against the worsening economy. Worse still, with the sale of that ancient heirloom, the last vestiges of our dignity and familial prestige went out the door. You were so fortunate to have left when you did. As for me, I am willing to emigrate if you could find some employment for your obedient servant and his offspring, since I am a firm believer in the poet's wise dictum, to wit, "Dying a death of misery is too high a price to pay for allegiance to one's ancestral land." He had signed his letter officiously, both in Persian and Latin scripts, and had affixed to it his business seal: "Haj Mahdi Darbani & Co."

Mr. Alpha had so far received a total of fifty-six letters from home. He had stuffed them in his pillowcase, and at night, in the dim isolation of his room he listened to the muffled crinkling noise they made in his ear. The noise successively invoked the musty warmth of Mrs. Nabovat's breath, the noisy vibrancy of his students on the school grounds, the cool of Tehran summer nights laden with the fragrance of petunias in the front yard. He drifted to the visions of the moon sailing past the tall aspens and the craggy heights of the Alborz, the sun-filled houses, dusty lanes. In his nocturnal fantasies, Mr. Alpha was transported to his ancestral home and the neighborhood in which he had grown up. Within the safe radius of these old remembrances of hereditary forms and native tribal sounds, he felt himself in a secure orbit in which he could sleep. He could dream of summer orchards and mule-trains and visualize himself in a temporal and spatial perspective in which his humanity was immune to the distorting effects of being an outsider in a foreign land.

For his part, Mr. Alpha had written letters home. "I am lost and bewildered here," he had said in one of them to Mr. Fazeli, the chemistry teacher. "I do not understand things and my behavior is often misunderstood. I do not seem to be able to break through the barriers I find in my path every day. My past is all lost to me, and my vision of the future does not extend beyond the end of the week. Every day, I do something that violates the local custom, and something untoward happens daily: I lose money, I misplace my keys, I run into things. I often have a strong feeling that I have been transformed into somebody else, as though I am standing in a hall of distorting mirrors and everything about me is deformed and grotesque. Sometimes I even doubt my mental health and fear that in this foreign atmosphere I may lose the meager balance of my sanity."

To another colleague, Mr. Milani the English teacher, he had confessed his profound bewilderment: "I simply do not understand how and why I was propelled so far off-base. I am totally at a loss as to how it all came about. Believe me, as a teacher of history, I never expected to be a part of it and hoped that, for its part, history would also pass me by."

In retrospect, everything was the fault of his students, the students he had cherished and nurtured to the best of his ability. Had they not issued a "death warrant" against him, things would have been different. If on that fateful day they had not thrown that massive rock from an upstairs class window at his head, he would have never ended up in this god-forsaken land. He would have remained back in Tehran among his friends and with his beloved Mrs. Nabovat.

But the fact remained that the rock had been aimed at his head by a student and it had left a nasty gash that had taken sixteen sutures to close. The scar was still raw and sore to the touch. Yet, he could not believe that it had really happened. But he was reminded of its reality every time he touched it and winced in discomfort.

The question of which student had thrown the rock gnawed at him constantly. He always prided himself on how well he got along with his students. He had often told Mrs. Nabovat that he considered them as his own children. "They are the birds in my bower," he told her. He was sincerely committed to their welfare and development, and during the febrile days of the revolution he had worried for their safety. He would not rest until he had accounted for every one of them. It was out of concern that he had followed them in their marches and demonstrations and chanted their slogans. It was for them that he mouthed uncomprehendingly abstractions about freedom and independence. He wanted a better tomorrow for them and it was for them that he sought the vague notions of the revolution.

Now he wanted to put everything behind him. He did not mention their names and fought off the memories of those days of encounter and conflict. But he would dream of them at night and would wake up racked with emotional pain. The hurt was in his heart, and it wrested from him whatever equanimity he could muster.

The bitterness that resulted from the rock-throwing incident swayed him in favor of his uncle's rhetoric, which equated patriotic zeal with nostalgia for the distant past. To long for the glories of the past, he said, is like making love to a cadaver; it brings forth nothing.

Even Mrs. Nabovat had urged him to venture out of the familiar rut. "March forth and seek out new horizons. Perhaps something novel will come your way and you will stumble on something worthwhile."

He had decided they were right—nothing ventured, nothing gained. He had another forty years of his life ahead of him, years which, broken down into seconds, would comprise millions of units of the future, a future which held the promise of a better life. Therefore, to hell with the past, he had decided. To hell with tribal and familial bonds, with ancestral land and memories attached to it. He had convinced himself that it was time to snap the tether of inherited culture and everything that tied him down to the burden of the past. He was now determined to enter a new dimension of time and space and inaugurate a new history with fresh thoughts and pristine experience.

From the outside, Mr. Alpha could hear a loud and belligerent voice, which he immediately recognized as that of the concierge having an altercation with the Indian tenant who occupied the room directly below Mr. Alpha's. He gazed at the door in awe, half expecting it to burst open. He could not make out anything of the confusion of voices permeating his room, but he was certain a house rule had been violated and this frightened him. Perhaps a stupid tenant had forgotten to shut the front door; or somebody, even more confused and disoriented than he, had left a trash bag at the foot of the stairs. Perhaps he himself had committed an infraction of the rules. He could not remember anything with certainty, but he was known to have forgotten to turn off the light in the bathroom and on occasion had absentmindedly tossed a cigarette butt in the yard. These transgressions were invariably reported to the Madame Concierge who would rush upstairs to Mr. Alpha's room and scream admonitions and threats at him, while he squirmed with embarrassment and hopelessly tried to explain that he came from a good and respectable family and owned a house in Tehran of stately proportions and attributes, and that it was out of necessity that he had to live in such reduced circumstances. But his knowledge of French fell miserably short of what he meant to convey, and his desperate groping for words was always interpreted as an admission of guilt.

The dispute went on, and he listened to the inarticulate pleas of the Indian and felt himself a codefendant in the blame directed at him. As an animal in danger, he retracted his legs to his chest and withdrew to a corner of the bed. He tried to shut out the noise emanating from the downstairs hall by thinking of pleasant things, such as the first day of school, of those halcyon days when children came back from summer holidays dressed in new clothes wearing shining shoes and carrying fresh books. On that day, teachers usually congregated in the principal's small office. There would be political discussions, Mr. Fazeli's old tired jokes and the principal's cock-and-bull stories, the stench of cheap perfume arising from Mrs. Cheraghi the math teacher, and, of course, Seyyed, the school janitor/servant, perennially serving tea and sweet toast to the staff. He was reminded of the first snow of the year, which would cover the entire city in white and muffled the usual school-yard sounds. On those cold days, hot tea was so especially welcome. He could taste the last gulp, heavily sugared and mixed with the dregs of the sweet toast that he always dunked in his tea. Staff members circling the kerosene heater, wistfully silent, the school and the whole town quieted down with snow. His thoughts then drifted to Mrs. Nabovat, her flowered skirt and sneakers, the wide leather belt, the gilded buttons of her shirt and the ever-present whistle around her neck which seemed almost a part of her anatomy. Alireza Nabovat, her husband, used to say that his wife's whistle was like the Archangel's trumpet: it would continue to blow till the Resurrection Day! The sound of that whistle reverberated in Mr. Alpha's ear, and he took it as a harbinger of her letter waiting for him in the mail box. The prospect of receiving Mrs. Nabovat's letter always titillated Mr. Alpha.

Usually, Mr. Alpha did not open Mrs. Nabovat's letters right away. He would meticulously fold them and put them in his pocket and go on about his daily rounds. He would do his shopping and go to the bank or post office. Then, he would take a leisurely walk along the river front. Sometimes, if his meanderings took him past a church, he would go in and light a candle. Throughout his walk. he would be excitedly conscious of the small weight of the envelope in his breast pocket. Back in his room, he would maintain the unhurried, elaborate tempo of his movements: washing his hands, taking his shoes and clothes off and putting them away neatly, tidying up the room, even dusting his meager possessions. He invariably pulled a chair close to the window and lit a cigarette and sipped on a glass of water before gently and ceremoniously producing the lightly perfumed letter from his pocket and settling down to read it. He held the letter in his hand as a devout believer would a holy relic. His eyes gloated over it with loving ecstasy. He paused at every crossed-out word and studied every ink spot. He found special meanings in every indentation. Sometimes he passed over certain paragraphs, leaving them for a more opportune moment to read, expecting that they would afford more joy later. He let the words echo in his mouth and allowed his tongue to wrap around them. With his eyes closed, he let the meaning of every word penetrate the very depth of his existence. He read Mrs. Nabovat's letters over and over again and found new connotations in every reading. His senses physically responded to the significance of every word, and he actually swallowed the sentences as he would a holy sacrament.

Mr. Alpha's worst days were rainy days, especially if he found his mail box empty. He would then be at a loss for the rest of the day. He would wander aimlessly up and down the street, or sit in a cafe and watch the people he did not know, or make useless attempts to read the newspaper. In his room, he would mope around, washing clothes, darning socks, sewing on a loose button. He often took an early refuge in his bed. In a letter, his uncle had intimated that solitude in exile is preferable to disenfranchisement at home. "My dear nephew," he had written, "in my home town I feel more foreign than a total stranger, and more segregated than a leper. I am at a loss whether to stay or leave. Even if I decide to leave, I have nowhere to go."

It was time to get out of bed. The morning had almost half gone by. Languishing in bed was a new development in Mr. Alpha's habits. All his life he had been an early riser. He even did not allow tardy students in class. But now he had become listless and indolent, staying in bed long hours and dozing off frequently. He felt as if he had been transformed into someone else, someone he did not particularly like. He was afraid that he might be suffering from split personality. He was afraid that his thoughts might take a different course and his aspirations change. He had started to distrust his memories. He sustained a deep anxiety that his foreign sojourn, like an acid, would corrode his "Mr. Alpha-ness." And yet, he did not know what to do about all this. Life beyond the windowpanes seemed to have no relation to him, and events were beyond his control. As if every incident happened when his back was turned. The bed was the only place that offered safety and warmth against an unsympathetic world. He prolonged his stay in bed, and there, whirling among memories, he reviewed the interminable impressions he had of Mrs. Nabovat: Mrs. Nabovat, the kind and caring physical education instructor at Shapoor High School, demonstrating a jump, tossing a ball, blowing her little whistle, chiming in with the students in singing the morning hymn. He visualized Mrs. Nabovat when he had known her as a strapping young woman with long, black hair, healthy white teeth—invulnerable and energetic, poised to tackle life with vitality and zest.

And Mrs. Nabovat as the tomboyish little girl next door, now riding her tricycle recklessly in the street, now hanging perilously from the tree branches, always boisterous, forever chasing along walls and rooftops. He remembered his exasperation at this girl. Sometimes he had the urge to beat her, puncture the tires of her tricycle, snatch her ball or drag her along by her braids. And sometimes, in contrast, he wanted to give her all his marbles, crayons, and his collection of dried flowers and foreign stamps. He wanted to do her homework and carry her satchel, weighted down with an unimaginable assortment of knick-knacks, all the way to the school. In warm weather the little girl often played in the shallow pool of her house. She was plumpish and well rounded, and her wavy hair cascaded down her face and shoulders. Along the side of the pool, she set her menagerie of critters, which at different times included such specimens as a week-old chick, a lizard, a turtle, a spider, a silkworm in its cocoon, all kept in their respective boxes. Sometimes, she washed the chick with soap and water or tied a string to the legs of a hapless moth and let it flip-flop in the water. She would take a dive or turn somersaults and point a pejorative finger at him and laugh gleefully while he, scrawny, unathletic, and deathly scared of water, withdrew in mortification behind tubs of pickles ranged in a row on the veranda. He produced Mrs. Nabovat's last letter from under his pillow. It was pages long. He started covering his body with the sheets of paper—his face, abdomen, thighs—and drifted off into the recollections of the day of his departure.

There she was, Mrs. Nabovat, behind the plate-glass wall of the airport lobby. Her cheeks were wet with tears. It was Monday, the eleventh of October. Mrs Nabovat made gestures and shouted words that were lost in the distance. She had arrived too late and could not be admitted to the transit lounge. She had pushed her way to the glass wall and was beating on it with her fist. From behind the airport building, Mr. Alpha could hear sporadic small-arms fire. A state of general pandemonium prevailed all over the airport. A bomb had been reported on board one of the planes, and there was a rumor that some foreign crew members had been abducted. Passengers were mulling around haphazardly rushing towards any door that would open. An elderly woman had passed out on the staircase, and a young man hovered despondently over her, pleading with the guards, policemen, airline officials, or anyone who would listen for seats on board the aircraft. There were pieces of unclaimed luggage in the middle of the hall, and the security personnel in the midst of this commotion were looking for a suspect, checking passports and travel papers. Mrs. Nabovat by now had reached the window and was pressing against it, motionless. From behind the smudged panes, her face looked like an ancient likeness glazed on an antique piece of ceramic. They were calling the passengers to the gates and he had to hurry, shoving and pulling his overstuffed and heavy handbags.

The worst part was the body search. He had to strip, even take off his shoes and socks, to open his mouth wide and stick out his tongue. The inspector poked a stick in his hair and peeked in his underwear. His shoulder pads were too large. There was another official standing by with a pair of scissors. He wished he could just turn back. So what if a student had broken his head? These were the days of rock-throwing and head-smashing. Being near Mrs. Nabovat was worth more than any equanimity foreign residence could offer. Paris was just not his kind of town. What was it that was forcing him to leave home? Who or what was he trying to escape? The fault was that of his students. No, it was the fault of the Shah who had abandoned everything and left the country. Or was it the fault of the people? Or foreign intrigue?

In the final analysis, it was his own fault for being indecisive and vague about his own ideals. Somehow, he had trusted the revolution and had construed it as the judgment of the masses and a historical imperative. He had contributed blankets and medical supplies, even a liter of his blood for the care of the wounded, a whole month's wages to the striking journalists. He had felt proud that his neglected nation was at long last the cynosure of world attention. For once, he had felt that he had a hand in shaping events and making things happen. Although he had never considered himself a man of religious convictions, yet his heart pounded to the reverberations of "Allah Akbar,"[1] shouted by a myriad of voices from rooftops. He had always been a defender of reason and exact sciences vis-à-vis religious sentiment. He had even allowed himself moments of doubt in the existence of an almighty god. With friends and associates, he always argued from a materialistic premise. With his students, he often discoursed on the implacability of history and social tenets. He viewed himself as a progressive who shunned the arbitrariness of religious ritual. And now, he was baffled by this surge of religious feeling in himself. He could not understand the force that swayed him, against all his commitment to the dictates of reason, toward god and appurtenances of religious faith. Mr. Alpha had even participated in the Friday mass prayer. That day, he had walked all over the city and arrived at the university campus at the time of Namaz.[2] Men and women of all ages went through the motions of the ritual in unison. He was positioned next to a mere boy and followed him as he performed the Namaz. He was confused and inept, but that did not seem to matter. In the past, the sight of his father at prayer had depressed him, and he invariably skipped the house when his mother hosted religious ceremonies at home. He loathed the mullahs and encouraged his students to heed the lessons of history and study Marx and physical sciences. But now, participation in the events had caused a drastic and incomprehensible change, as if he was possessed or spellbound.

He had joined Ashoora[3] demonstrations along with students, friends, neighbors, and colleagues, all except Mrs. Nabovat. Streets were soon packed with crowds who would arrive in small groups amidst shouts of

"Allah-o-Akbar," some of them beating their breasts rhythmically, some others beating their backs and shoulders with chains. The girls, clad in full Islamic garb, held hands and chanted a mournful strain. Street urchins draped in shrouds followed them, along with old women and some disabled men in wheelchairs. This procession produced more noise than the rest.

To Mr. Alpha, it was the Day of Resurrection, and the air was redolent with the smell of Imam Hussein's blood and the blood of all the victims of injustice. Some women carried placards displaying pictures of their martyred sons, and men in funereal black beat their fists to their breast. A cacophony of sorrow and lamentation filled the air with frequent slogans condemning the bloodthirsty Zazeed[4] and traitorous shah. Mr. Alpha was dragged-along uncontrollably in the middle of a large crowd. He was not familiar with the pervasive political and religious slogans, and yet, he felt invigorated and refreshed in his harmony with the boisterous throng. He had a sense of being a part of something unique and perfect. The myriad of sounds echoed inside his skull and, uncomprehending, he mouthed snatches of the things he heard. He was beside himself with the fever of mass hysteria and experienced a mysterious joy in being a part of a monolithic whole. He recalled that, in harmony with the crowd, he had whispered "Allah-o-Akbar" a few times and that had given him a surprising sense of release from all the inhibitions that had kept him in check all his life. From the depths of his guts, a shout had risen to his lips that gave vent to all the resentment and suffering of his life. It was a savage, primordial shout, which arose from all the pain and fear he had endured since childhood and had been instilled in his psyche as a member of the human race. But it also gave expression to the love that he bore Mrs. Nabovat and the tenderness he felt for her.

For Mr. Alpha, this was a totally unique experience. It was rumored in the family circles that he had not even cried at birth. In fact, he had been taken for a still-birth at first. In later life, he hardly ever made any protests against injustices done to him. He never made any attempts to defend himself when his brothers blamed him for their own mischief for which his father had often taken the belt to him. The groans of pain and bitterness formed in the extremities of his body and tangled up in his entrails and choked his breath. But he never allowed them to escape his lips. They remained, unseen and undetectable, in the untraversed crevices of his spirit.

Bibi-Khanum, his mother's aunt, was the only person who had shown any real affection to Mr. Alpha as a child. It was she who had comforted him after each whipping episode and attended to his bruises and contusions. It was Bibi Khanum who told him stories at bed-time and applied sugar beet extract to his raw, weather-chapped hands and administered home remedies to the warts around his neck. In her attempts to assure his health, she had fed him large spoonfuls of cod-liver oil every morning. Bibi-Khanum also gave him his monthly baths on the last Friday of every month in the neighborhood public bathhouse. His recollections of the monthly event were shrouded in the thick vapors of the heated pool in the bathhouse. The participants in these regular outings were often his mother, various and sundry aunts, his ursine girl cousins, some old women, and the younger Guiti-Khanum—the engineer's wife—and Miss Shokufeh, the seamstress. His impressions of these scenes were of bare, ample flesh, and the smell of henna, intermingled with the aroma of ice-cold refreshments and homemade snacks. The shrill voices of those women still echoed in his ear, distorted by the passage of years. Bibi-Khanum had bathed him meticulously. She washed and scrubbed every inch of his body. She made mounds of lather with the washcloth with which she rubbed him all over. She worked on his ears to the point of pulling them off and then rinsed them with hot water and disinfectant. She even scrubbed his heels with pumice. Then, in compliance with the religious requirements of cleanliness, she submerged him seven times in the near-boiling water of the heated pool till he almost drowned. Then he was thoroughly dried with what felt like the most abrasive towels in the world and dressed in so many layers of clothing that he could barely walk. And finally, when he felt completely exhausted and lifeless, he was revived by the cool taste of juice from a pomegranate that Bibi-Khanum squeezed in his mouth. Painfully crude and rough as she was in her touch, Bibi-Khanum was maternal and affectionate, always regarding him with a benign eye and sending him home with an earnest prayer after the bathing routine.

Later on, when he was older, he took his monthly baths with his father. He would sit in a corner of the bathhouse rotunda alone and unsmiling. His brothers, too, in the foreboding presence of their stern father, would be quiet and well-behaved. Nobody played or talked. His father's bathhouse cronies were all aged men with dilapidated bodies, ready to die. His father took cold showers and left the window open. As they went through the bathing ritual, the father would sermonize his shivering sons on the wiliness of Satan and the horrors of hell. He talked at length on the nature of sin and transgression. Sometimes, aroused into a frenzy by his own oratory, he would indiscriminately slap one of his sons across the face. He believed that crying had a cathartic effect on the spirit and was salutary to ocular hygiene. Even as a mere child, Mr. Alpha had speculated on saying or doing something to register protest. Now, older and an adolescent, he could have just left his father's presence. At least, he could have asserted himself by closing the window or turning on the hot water tap. He could have raised his hand to intercept his father's blows. But he had always suppressed the urge to do any of these things, always remaining submissive and silent, always postponing objections to paternal inclemencies to a later date.

Characteristically, Mr. Alpha had not opened up his heart to that childhood playmate, the girl next-door who later became Mrs. Nabovat, at a time when it mattered. He should have walked up to her and told her he loved her—pure and simple. Instead, he had watched her longing, expectant glances and her erratic and restless behavior. He watched her almost pine away in anticipation of his approach. He watched her throw tantrums and smash his cherished flower pots and ostentatiously flirt with Alireza Nabovat. He witnessed her dancing flauntingly at family parties with everyone, even the people she had not formally met. He saw her laughing loudly and self-consciously, showing off her engagement ring to all, but more specifically to him. He watched her in those gatherings as she stuffed herself with mounds of dried fruit and other snacks, which he knew she would be vomiting out an hour later in the bathroom. Mr. Alpha saw all of this and yet he kept his distance from the girl and never gave her any inkling of his own feelings. In retrospect, he knew that if he had mustered his courage and talked to the girl, everything would have been different—his life, her life, Alireza Nabovat's life, even the trajectory of that rock that hit him on that cursed day. Who knows, perhaps the entire course of world history would have changed for all concerned!

There was a knock on the door. Mr. Alpha, still helplessly adhering to the early morning drowsiness, dismissed it as a figment of his imagination. But it was no use, the wakeful part of his consciousness was now curious as to the identity of the guest waiting in the hall outside his door. Who could it be? Was it the concierge with another complaint? Or perhaps a new arrival from Iran? Mr. Alpha got up and staggered toward the door. He stepped on something sharp, which sent a shooting pain through his body. He put on his glasses and started looking for his slippers—with no success. How could he manage to lose everything in that confined space? Hurriedly, he looked behind the drapes and under the bed. He picked up a pair of slacks off the floor and shook them before laying them on the back of a chair. A handful of small change was scattered all over the floor. He glanced around the room and at his own appearance and felt a pang of depression. There were newspapers and books lying around, and every ashtray was brimming with cigarette butts. How untidy and slovenly he had become! He was now only a distant likeness of his former self. Mr. Alpha had always been clean and tidy to the point of compulsiveness. His clothes were always clean and crisply pressed. His small house was immaculate. Even his classroom was a model of tidiness and organization. He had made sure that his thoughts were in strict accordance with rules of logic and his plans thoroughly thought out. He could not remember the exact hour, day, or month when this drastic change of habit and character had set in.

There was the knock again, this time somewhat louder than before. Mr. Alpha abandoned his ruminations and started toward the door, but hesitated again, racked with the uncertainty as to who it might be. His heart was beating erratically, and he had a strange urge to run away. Who could be behind that door? Words formed on his lips but faded before he could utter them. He listened intently, hoping to divine the identity of the caller by the noises from the hall. But there were no sounds. Perhaps it was the mailman, trying to deliver a registered letter. In his agitation, Mr. Alpha could not speculate any more. By now, he wished to crawl back into his bed or throw open a window and gasp for breath. But he was immobilized by a nameless fear and stood motionless in the middle of the room with his eyes glued on the door. Could it be Mrs. Nabovat? Ridiculous. Impossible. But why not? This was not totally outside the realm of possibility. The vagaries of fate are such that bliss and disaster are separated by just a hairline. What if Mrs. Nabovat was behind that door? He would be seized by a paroxysm of joy. He would let out a deafening yell, beat his head on the nearest wall, and swoon in her arms. But no. More characteristically, in a sonorous and distant tone, he would announce: "I will be with you in a minute. Please wait." During the time that this announcement brought him, he would brush his teeth, shave, dress suitably, and tidy up the room before answering the door. All this time, his beloved Mrs. Nabovat would be standing in the hall, getting impatient and flustered. She would perhaps suspect that he was entertaining a guest, a French or Iranian woman. In a fit of jealousy, she would perhaps give up and leave. There was another knock on the door, less resolute and indicative of the caller's giving up the hope of response.

Mr. Alpha bolted forward and reached for the doorknob. But he withdrew his hand, seized with hesitation. In his ear, the knock had a heavy and impatient echo, not like the gentle rap of a lover's hand, not like the soft and tender touch of Mrs. Nabovat. This knock sounded cold, brutal, and aggressive. Through the crack of the ill-fitting door, he could feel the biting cold blowing in. His nostrils were attuned to detect the familiar fragrance of Mrs. Nabovat from miles away; there was nothing but the winds of Europe blowing in the hallway. What fantasy had overtaken him! Mrs. Nabovat in Paris! He must be losing his sanity to think such things. He was sure it was because of being in constant suspense, in a limbo between a distant past and a dim future. At last, Mr. Alpha thought of peeping through the keyhole. All he could see was a pair of a woman's legs clad in black hose and in a masculine-looking pair of shoes. Slowly he opened the door. Standing in the corridor was an older woman, short and stocky, perhaps an old nurse or a nun. "Bonjour," she said and rattled off a long sentence in French. She had a strange accent, and Mr. Alpha did not understand a word of what she said. He blushed in embarrassment and gave an ambiguous shake of his head, followed by a laugh, which he immediately felt was untimely and improper. Hurriedly, he recomposed his face in an attempt to look serious. The woman repeated her sentence and produced a few post cards from a dingy, soiled envelope. There were color pictures of Christ, Mary, and Notre Dame. Mr. Alpha had read *The Hunchback of Notre Dame* and held Victor Hugo in special regard. He took the pictures and pointed at the Notre Dame with a gesture that he hoped conveyed his admiration. He detected a flicker of comprehension in the woman's eyes and felt some satisfaction in having established a rapport with her. He then pointed to his pajamas meaning to apologize for his inappropriate dress. The woman looked at him with indifference.

Mr. Alpha was desperately trying to compose a sentence to fit the occasion, but all he could remember was the last lesson in his high-school French, which had to do with calling a porter at the railway station. The woman took a handkerchief from her pocket and blew her nose. Mr. Alpha reviewed the pictures once again and read aloud the captions under each one. It occurred to him that perhaps the woman was trying to sell the postcards. But he immediately castigated himself for even thinking it. She was obviously from a holy order on a mission to propagate Christianity and bring succor and solace to displaced, homeless persons. She would be offended if he offered money in return for the postcards. The woman had more pictures, which she handed to Mr. Alpha. He pointed to a picture of the crucifix and tried to give his face an expression of respect and compassion. "I am an Iranian, a Muslim," he said, assuming that the woman would understand his predicament. He then heaved a sigh and stood aside, ushering the woman into the room. He even permitted himself to give the woman a friendly tap on the shoulder. But the woman did not move. Mr. Alpha insisted. He then moved to the far end of the room and placed a picture of Christ in the corner of a mirror on the wall. The woman walked in reluctantly and sat on the only chair in the room. As soon as she sat down, she started rubbing her knee, apparently in pain. Mr. Alpha said something apologetic about the appearance of the room. Hastily, he tried to make the bed and then picked up a bundle of newspapers off the floor and hid them behind a curtain. This was the first time that a French person had visited his room in a spirit other than protest or chastisement .

"Would you care for some tea? Iranian tea? Scheherazade tea?" Mr. Alpha asked. The woman firmly shook her head in negation. From a suitcase, he produced a box of Iranian confectionary, and as unobtrusively as he could, he flicked off a dead beetle stuck to its bottom and offered it to the woman. She cast a hesitant glance at the contents but took one and kept it in her fist. Mr. Alpha shoved the box toward her in a gesture of insistence that she should take some more. He then filled the kettle and put it on the hot plate. He stuffed a piece of candy in his mouth and, by sucking on it noisily, tried to convey to the woman that it tasted good.

The woman, however, had no intention of eating the candy. She turned her head and silently stared at the map of Iran on the wall. Then she adjusted her glasses and peered at the picture of Mrs. Nabovat in a frame on the bedside table and the small Persian rug on the floor.

Mr. Alpha was preparing himself to deliver a disquisition on the art of carpet weaving in Iran when the woman suddenly stood up. Obviously, she was late and had to be on her way. Mr. Alpha, on the other hand, was beginning to relax and was looking forward to a chat with this newfound friend. But then, he reminded himself of the fact that Europeans have a special view of time and are unwilling to waste it in inconsequential talk, that they are very cautious and conservative and do not generally confide in strangers. But, that did not matter; Mr. Alpha could wait for future meetings. The woman put on her thick gloves and put away the piece of candy in her handbag. In an abrupt and impatient tone she said: "Fifty francs for the five postcards." Mr. Alpha understood what she said but could not believe his ears. The surprise interrupted his train of thought. He felt he was getting red in the face and his eyes were bulging out of his head. He tried desperately to contain the welter of rage and disillusionment that swelled within him. He wanted to return the postcards and summarily turn the woman out of the room. But, he knew immediately that that was beyond him. He was simply too timid, and he would be mortified to do something like that. Involuntarily, he extended his hand towards the woman as if he wanted to shake hers, but then hastily stuffed it in his pocket. Lost for words, he tugged nervously at a thread in his pocket. The thread would not snap. He rolled it around a finger and pulled harder.

"Fifty francs for five postcards," the woman repeated dryly, thinking that perhaps she had not been understood.

Mr. Alpha could not bring himself to pay. His anger stemmed from a sense of betrayal and a feeling that his intelligence had been insulted. But how could he get out of the situation with any grace? All he had with him was a 200-franc bill. Perhaps, he could plead lack of change and ask her to come some other time. But even that would compromise his dignity. He produced the large bill and held it out to the woman. She grabbed the money, changed it, and took fifty francs out of it. She returned the rest to Mr. Alpha, thanked him perfunctorily, and left.

Mr. Alpha closed the door and stood in the middle of the room indecisively. The kettle had come to a boil and was bubbling on the hotplate. He felt a sudden flash of heat and took off his housecoat. There was a burning sensation in his stomach and a dull anxiety circulated in his body. He felt as if a heavy load was pressing his shoulders and bending his spine. He caught sight of a beetle that was climbing on the candy box, one of many pests that had infested the whole tenement and were not deterred by his faint attempts at spraying. It occurred to him to change his abode on account of the infestation. As he aimed a book at the intruding beetles, he caught a glimpse of the picture of Jesus Christ and was filled with a surge of anger. Next time, he promised himself, he would open the door and shout at the vendors. He would not let the vendors open their mouths. He would even resort to violence if they persisted. Should this bring the concierge up to his floor, so much the better. He wouldn't care even if the police were called. He would even beat and abuse the constable.

But then, it was all his own fault. He could have refused to buy the cursed wares. A simple "no" would have sufficed. He could even have said "no" to Alireza Nabovat. "No, I won't let you have my bicycle. It is mine and I need it." But, he never could refuse to give in. So he had to run after Alireza and the little-girl-next-door, who would happily pedal up the road and giggle at his attempts to keep up with them on foot. The little-girl-next-door, by the way, jealously guarded her own bike and would not allow anyone to touch it, let alone borrow it.

On Fridays and other public holidays, the three of them played in the hills of Elahieh. Alireza and the little-girl-next-door often racing ahead on bicycles and Mr. Alpha following them in leaps and bounds all the way down to the bottom of the hill. There, Alireza would take his shirt off and lie flat on the bottom of the little stream running along the path. Alireza's boyish physique was firm and sculptured, and Mr. Alpha thought at the time, and even in later years, that a youth with a body like that deserved all the bicycles and perhaps all the women in the world, including the little-girl-next-door.

Usually on the way back, Alireza would give Mr. Alpha his bicycle, and as the three of them walked back up the hill, he would place his hand on Mr. Alpha's shoulder. Mr. Alpha would feel a current of warmth and friendship flow into his body. At parting, the girl would divide between them little, tart, unripe plums she had gathered from the trees along the route. She would furtively give Mr. Alpha three or four more than she had set aside for Alireza. Those summer afternoons were times of unparalleled happiness.

The distant toll of church bells could be heard again: it must be close to mid-day. Mr. Alpha drew a deep breath and twisted his stiff neck. The ambient humidity had penetrated his vertebrae and made him long for the heat of the sun, the radiant sun of the desert that impacted the skull with sword-like sharpness. Mr. Alpha shuffled to the window and looked out. A shaft of sunlight had illuminated the upper layer of clouds, and there were children playing in the nearby public garden. He could hear some birds chirping under the gables of the neighboring building, and it dawned on him that it was the third day after the vernal equinox. Despite the chill in the air, Mr. Alpha felt that the earth had now emerged from the winter gloom, and the thought of impending spring and summer gave him a surge of euphoria. "Everything will turn out fine," he muttered-to himself. "All that's needed is patience and faith." He involuntarily glanced at the picture of Jesus Christ. The picture appeared to stare back at him benignly. Exactly at this point, his eye caught a glimpse of the lost slipper and, with that, what was left of his anger and chagrin dissipated completely. He even decided to take the visit of the old woman as a sign of good omen. He threw open the window and, although a biting cold breeze assailed his nostrils, he drew several deep breaths. "If the Lord in his infinite wisdom chooses to close a door," Mr. Alpha remembered the old adage, "in his boundless mercy he will open a window elsewhere."

And suddenly, in a rush of enthusiasm and energy, he decided to tidy up his room. He first attacked the pile of dishes left over from many a past dinner. He washed them all slowly and meticulously. He then made up his bed and neatly placed Mrs. Nabovat's letters under his pillow. After watering his solitary geranium, he organized his breakfast tray. He performed all these tasks as cautiously and noiselessly as possible to avoid making any sounds as he walked on the floor or opened and closed cabinet doors. In the first days of his arrival, intent on feeling good and fortunate, he always got up early and opened the window. Leaving his door ajar in anticipation of an unexpected visitor or well-wisher, he listened to his radio and whistled while he shaved. Sometimes, he made tea in the little samovar he had brought with him from home and put various boxes of candy on display in order to facilitate the approach by a prospective friend among the neighbors. The practice, however, had only resulted in acrimonious complaints to the concierge by the residents next door and on the lower floor. The concierge had in turn sent him threatening notices, admonishing him to desist in making so much noise. Thereafter, Mr. Alpha kept his door and windows closed and drank his tea in silence. He even stopped his calisthenics or limited them to lying-down exercises and the twist of the neck.

From down below at the street level, Mr. Alpha heard the concierge talking to her dog. She addressed the animal in affectionate terms, giving it counsel, or so it sounded to Mr. Alpha. The woman treated the dog erratically. Sometimes she would ignore it and its whining. At other times, she would take it in her arms and wipe its nose and adorn its ears and tail with colorful bows. The dog itself was unattractive and foul-tempered. It positively disliked Mr. Alpha and set up a howl whenever he was near. Perhaps, the memory of a discrete kick Mr. Alpha had given it at one time was forever fresh in its mind. The concierge, suspicious of the animosity the dog felt toward Mr. Alpha, would always gather the animal in her arms and eye him doubtfully as he passed by. Mr. Alpha, pretending he did not notice there was anything the matter, would stride by, tip his hat at the concierge, wave at the grunting dog, and bolt through the front door.

The mailman always came around noon. Mr. Alpha, therefore, packed his breakfast things and left the breadcrumbs on the ledge for the pigeons. He got dressed, locked the door, and went down the staircase. He did not turn on the light in the corridor, since he did not wish to be noticed. The mailbox was empty. A sudden rush of anxiety overtook him, and a series of worrisome thoughts raced through his mind. But he managed to ward off depression and attributed the undue concern to his loneliness and the consistently overcast skies of Europe. Instead, he forced his attention to the coming of spring and the charming row of budding, red tulips adorning the sides of the path. He couldn't help wondering why nobody ever tried to pick them at night. "What civic-minded people," he thought to himself. "I did the right thing in coming here."

Feeling unusually euphoric and buoyant, upon entering the small postal bureau, Mr. Alpha uttered a resounding "Bonjour," and after finishing his business walked briskly out. In the process, he ran into the glass door but did not allow the accident to disturb his aplomb. Once outside, he noticed the concierge walking in his direction. So he discretely walked to the other side of the street. Small school children were scattered all over the sidewalk on their way back from school. Some of them were lugging heavy satchels. It must be lunchtime, Mr. Alpha decided. Mr. Alpha occasionally stepped aside to let them pass. He could hear their tiny, sweet voices, which to his uncomprehending ear sounded like cooing of doves. Sometimes, upon running into groups of children, Mr. Alpha would try to talk to them and offer them candy. If they stopped, he would affectionately pat them on the head or stroke their hair. If they let him, he would kneel down to do an occasional button or tie up a loose shoestring. He had a strong desire to see their notebooks and go over their homework and mark it with red pen. Not very far away, Mr. Alpha could hear the barking of the concierge's dog. So he quickened his pace and stopped at a news agent's kiosk. He picked up a magazine and thumbed casually through it before putting it down. He then picked up a newspaper and turned to the rental housing notices. He was half thinking of moving. One or two of the rooms advertised caught his attention. He quickly produced his pen and a piece of paper and jotted down the phone numbers. The newsagent, who was quietly watching him all this time, mumbled something in protest. Mr. Alpha realized what he had done was not right. He felt some shame for having tried to get something for nothing. He smiled vaguely at the newsagent and looked at the price of the paper. It was prohibitive. Besides, he remembered that he had already spent fifty francs on the church and Jesus Christ. Somehow, the idea eased his conscience. So, he ignored the gaze of the vendor, turned around and got underway, already trying to plan how to spend the day. He thought of paying a new-year's visit to an Iranian colonel he had made friends with at the language class. The colonel was a fugitive from the revolution and did not have a dwelling of his own. He and his family temporarily resided at the lodgings of a young student who at one time had borrowed some money from Mr. Alpha and had so far not paid him back. Mr. Alpha was afraid that the young man might again accost him for more money. So he gave up on visiting the colonel. He wished he had brought his camera with him so he could take snapshots of all those historical edifices. And Mr. Fazeli had been begging him for pictures of Napoleon's mausoleum. The principal, on the other hand, had been asking for a certain intestinal-gas pain remedy. He did not know the name of the brand but had explained that it was a small, round, orange-colored tablet and a neighbor had been getting it from a relative in Paris who had bought it from a small pharmacy in the corner of L'Etoile. The neighbor had been taking those tablets right up to the time of his demise and, according to the principal, had died a painless and happy death. Mr. Alpha knew of a pharmacy on his own street but didn't know how to ask for a nameless drug without embarrassing himself. He had once accompanied an Iranian artillery colonel and his wife to a doctor's office. The couple's ailments were not translatable in any language: he suffered from a stomach that was "angry" and a persistent tingling sensation in his palms and the soles of his feet. She complained of an elusive discomfort in her heart and wanted him to explain to the doctor that there was no pain or palpitation, but that her heart would at times "go to pieces." Mr. Alpha did not know the equivalent of "go to pieces." So she would try to explain to the doctor herself that her heart stretched out like warm, malleable wax or chewing gum. The doctor stared at the three of them in profound bewilderment and rapidly jotted down notes on his pad.

A bus appeared at the end of the street. Mr. Alpha distanced himself from the woman standing near him at the bus stop in fear that she might try to strike up a conversation on the weather or the tardiness of the bus or her own personal problems. As usual, Mr. Alpha would miss most of what was being said and would have to beat his brains out guessing the drift of the conversation and make proper noises and gesticulations. These situations always took a heavy toll on his energies.

He got on the half-empty bus and took a window seat. He didn't have a particular destination in mind. So, he stretched out his legs and decided to go all the way to the end of the route. He would relax until he got off and made his way back on foot.

Paris was truly a beautiful city, Mr. Alpha thought. Row after row of monuments, mirrors, churches, steeples, museums and historical edifices, a plenary of goods and merchandise and an endless flow of words, books, magazines, foods and beverages. But, Paris was also full of loneliness and secret fears of death and impermanence. There were numberless dogs—dogs that in an odd way resembled human beings. To Mr. Alpha, Paris was a city of closed doors, hermetically sealed windows, and shutout eyes. The beauty of Paris surpassed anything human; it had the fearsome presence of a mysteriously magical Princess, arrogant in the certainty of her ever-lasting youth and beauty in the face of human mortality, at once charming and lethal, gracious and treacherous. That was perhaps the reason why Mr. Alpha harbored a deep-seated fear of this city. The Notre Dame, especially, was the focus of this fear. All that intricate, enigmatic and ancient beauty, with all those graven images of saints and demons took his breath away and he was awe-struck by the stony massiveness of the cathedral. To Mr. Alpha, that edifice was the material incarnation of all heaven and earth, where Jesus Christ had been nailed down to the floor of the universe. Somewhere in the dark shadows of the church, Mr. Alpha could envision his father and the childhood bathhouse scenes and could feel the floggings he had received at his hand. Invariably, the sight of the Notre Dame made Mr. Alpha ache for the bright sunshine of the Iranian desert and the open, unhampered plains—and for Bibi Khanum's gentle, affectionate touch. It was now three days past the vernal equinox, and a pale sun had momentarily eluded the heavy clouds. The reflections on the dusty expanse of a glass plate window formed themselves into shapes that in Mr. Alpha's eyes were that of Mrs. Nabovat seated at the traditional Iranian New Year's arrangement of spices and food items. She would be reading passages from his last letter to all those present. Mr. Alpha involuntarily lapsed into recollections of the New Year's Day ceremony of the last year and all those years before the revolution. There was Mother in the final stage of spring cleaning, he and his brothers all dressed up in new clothes, everything scrubbed clean and spotless in anticipation of the moment when it would be the new year—everyone in gay anticipation of better things and happier days to come. Bibi-Khanum was an ardent believer in a universal rebirth and catharsis every new year. She cleaned her house and bathed the children in preparation for the event. For several days before and after the New Year's Day she would sweep the yard and clean the front steps, sprinkling rose water everywhere in the belief that Khezr the Prophet,[5] concurrent with the New Year's festivities, would pass by the house. If she could catch a glimpse of him, all her wishes would be granted. In all those years as a growing boy, Mr. Alpha spent many a sleepless night in anticipation of a visit by Khezr around New Year's Day. He and Bibi-Khanum would be together in bed, awake and attentive to every little noise that came from the alley. Bibi-Khanum would feverishly recite the appropriate chants, and the little boy, with an expectant and palpitating heart, would gaze at the suggestive shapes formed by the shimmering shadows of trees. After he grew up, Mr. Alpha forgot about the Khezr story, but retained the habit of expecting something wonderful to happen on or around New Year's Day. He would still experience the anticipation and sweet anxiety, which kept him awake hours on end.

Mrs. Nabovat knew of this tendency in Mr. Alpha. "Darling," she had written to him with a tongue in cheek. "Don't lock your door. Who knows, perhaps the prophet is in your neighborhood. These days everybody is heading for Europe. Why not Khezr? We keep our house all closed up; we are not hoping for a visit. But it is different in your case. I still remember all those nights when you did not take your eyes off the front yard. Leave your doors open. You may yet have a visit from Khezr."

Traditionally, the seventh day after the New Year's was Mr. Alpha's turn to stay at home and receive visits from colleagues and students. The turn of Mrs. Cheraghi, the math teacher, was on the eleventh. Most teachers shunned her and found excuses to cancel their visit. Not the Nabovats and Mr. Alpha, though. They always stopped by to find a solitary and secretly chagrined Mrs. Cheraghi, who had made preparations for at least thirty people. Visibly embarrassed, Mrs. Cheraghi poured tea and served snacks and condiments, as her hands shook with a deep-seated anger, and her beady black eyes gleamed with visceral vindictiveness. She nevertheless held her head high and pretended to be in good humor. She would even find occasion to draw their attention to the picture of her fiancé, a police official assigned to a post in a provincial town, who was supposed to come to Tehran the following summer for the wedding. There had at least been ten such summers and the fiancé had not yet made the trip. The story was generally known around the school, and some waggish students would occasionally send bogus letters to Mrs. Cheraghi, which further inflamed her temper and made her take it out on the nearest students by hitting them with the sharp edge of a ruler and squeezing their fingers with a pencil between them or lifting them bodily by their earlobes.

The thirteenth day of the New Year was the traditional day for outings and family picnics. Mr. Alpha and his associates usually went to one of the resort areas in the countryside around Tehran. They usually left early. Mrs. Nabovat always took the wheel and drove recklessly. Alireza Nabovat stretched on the back seat and went to sleep instantly, unconcerned. But Mr. Alpha would stay awake, petrified with fears of impending annihilation. He made furious and futile gestures trying to wave the oncoming traffic out of the way, certain that they would all be pulverized by a tanker truck. In the course of the turbulent ride, he would hit his head and shoulders against the roof and windows of the car. Miraculously, they would all arrive at the destination in one piece and would immediately started unloading the picnic paraphernalia by the side of a stream. After a vigorous game of volleyball, they would all lie around and take a snooze before supper.

Mr. Alpha cherished those moments of semi-consciousness. He was marginally aware of what went on around him, but his spirit was elsewhere, somewhere empty and silent, in a serene hiatus between two fleeting moments. His body and mind would wind down almost to the point of entropy, and his thoughts, light airy bubbles, would emerge from unknown origins and drift into nothingness. His senses, honed to the delicacy of shadows dancing on the surface of a gentle stream, would relieve him of an invisible burden. It was as if he had a moment's reprieve from the passage of time and immunity from the hardships of life. It was an experience Mr. Alpha had come to know as the beatific state, the hour of repose, the time to kick one's shoes off and listen to the sweet silence of things.

By now, the bus had pulled up to the curb, and a few elderly American women got on. They wanted to go to the Place d'Opera and didn't know how. They asked the driver and queried the passengers. No one knew any English. Mr. Alpha seriously considered giving assistance, but could not muster any interest in the matter. He knew enough English to show off but was reluctant to draw attention to himself, what with the hostage-taking incident in Tehran still fresh on everyone's mind. What if he was asked who he was and where he came from? He would have to declare his nationality and had a vague fear of doing so. The women had a city map and a subway guide, which they noisily consulted. The French bus riders, silent and haughty, regarded them with disdain, seething with anger at the Americans' deficiency in French. Fully determined not to get involved, Mr. Alpha turned his face away from the scene, pulled up the collar of his raincoat, and opted for anonymity.

He had had reports of events in Tehran. He knew that Mrs. Cheraghi had become the standard-bearer of revolutionary women, that she frequently marched and shouted slogans against the United States, the Great Satan. She had even participated in a rock-throwing ritual at the American Embassy. Mr. Alpha had also heard of the principal's strange transformation; that he had cut off all his associations, except with Mrs. Cheraghi, and had regular nightly meetings with God. He had now come to consider everything as untouchable and accused his friends of satanic liaisons. All these developments had come about during the past year. All his friends, as the planets of a disintegrating galaxy, were propelled to unimaginable destinies. As if driven by a centrifugal force, they all had a compulsion to leave the homeland. All, that is, except the Nabovats.

But he had heard nothing of his students, his "fiery finches of revolution." He still ached to know the identity of the rock thrower and the underlying motive for that action. He vividly remembered the events of that day. He had been awakened early that morning by the ringing of the telephone around five o'clock. Who could it be? At the other end of the line, somebody breathed heavily into the mouthpiece but said nothing. His mother was already awake and milling around the house. The phone rang again, and again there was silence on the line. What a stupid joke, he thought. From the street, he could hear the muffled sounds of an argument among some Afghani wetbacks. Mr. Hakami, his neighbor, was watering his garden, his small pocket radio blaring. He remembered having had a cursory breakfast that morning before heading out for school at eight o'clock. Most classes had not convened that morning, and a state of disorder pervaded the school. Teachers, uncertain and confused, would straggle into the faculty lounge and try to make sense of the situation. Mrs. Cheraghi, in black headgear and thick socks, was standing by the steps pretending she had not seen him. His classroom was locked. There was a poster on the door. "TRAITOROUS TEACHERS SHALL BE EXECUTED." The poster screamed at him in large letters. On the wall, there was a sketch that faintly resembled him. "Which traitorous teachers?" he asked himself in disbelief and stared at the picture on the wall. He was seized by a sense of foreboding and a premonition of untoward developments. Students behaved oddly and clearly stayed out of his way. He caught a glimpse of some peeking at him through half-opened doors. Out In the yard Mr. Fazeli was pacing back and forth, and Mrs. Nabovat, oblivious to the strange atmosphere, was trying to round up some students and get a volleyball game going. There was no sign of the principal. He thought Mr. Fazeli was beckoning to him, so he started walking in his direction. On the way, he nodded a hello to Mrs. Nabovat. He stopped to light a cigarette. As he struck a match inside his cupped hands, his head exploded.

The rock had hit Mr. Alpha's skull just above the neck. For the first few seconds after the impact, he had completely blacked out. There was nothing but darkness and deathly silence. Then, a searing pain had started to permeate his vertebrae, and a stream of warm blood had seeped past his collar and run down his chest. He could see people but was unable to assimilate the significance of their motions. There was Mrs. Nabovat, running toward him and dragging a student by the wrist. There was Mr. Fazeli, his mouth hanging open and wearing an expression of befuddlement. A shaft of sunlight penetrated his eyelids and there were dark, pulsating circles everywhere. He had at first leaned against a tree but had slid an incline and was now lying on the ground, half dead, as if immobilized by an incubus in his sleep. His brain was inoperative, and he could not feel the beating of his heart. His head, heavy as a barrel of tar, had slumped into Mrs. Nabovat's bosom. The only external stimulus he had been able to recognize was the sharpness of Mrs. Nabovat's whistle poking him in the ear.

The man seated across from Mr. Alpha on the bus seemed to be watching him intently. Self-conscious and uncomfortable, Mr. Alpha fidgeted and passed an anxious hand over his fly. "What the hell is he looking at?" he asked himself. Agitated, Mr. Alpha produced a handkerchief and wiped his mouth and nose and then re-crossed his legs. He took out a French book and tried to concentrate on it. Not succeeding, he thumbed through it and then returned it to his pocket. For a while he thought of protesting to the man, but gave up on the idea, giving the man the benefit of a doubt. He did look dazed. He had seen a lot of Europeans in a daze, especially on busses and trains. Nevertheless, Mr. Alpha did not like to be stared at. It made him uneasy. So he got up and made his way toward the exit. In the process, he jostled a woman and stepped on another's toes—for which he apologized profusely. He practically burst out of the bus as soon as it stopped and let out a deep sigh of relief. He did not know where he was. But he didn't care. He could walk around, window shop, and kill some time. Ahead of him was a narrow, winding alley lined with antique shops and second hand stores. He started walking and stopped in front of a barbershop with a large mirror in the window. He was startled by his own reflection. He looked more closely. What a disgraceful appearance! He looked disheveled and derelict. His ill-fitting raincoat and a worn-out fur hat promoted a general air of disrepute. His complexion was decidedly swarthy and, together with his dark eyes and eyebrows, contrasted oddly with this gray mustache. He looked far from respectable, more like a burglar or a terrorist on the run. But his self-image was so different. He thought of himself as an attractive individual—distinguished and dignified, a teacher of history, a gentleman scholar, moderately known and generally well thought of. He had come to view himself through Mrs. Nabovat's amorous glance and his mother's loving eyes. He had always felt secure in the approval and admiration that he inspired in his circle of acquaintances. He even had an inkling that young high-school girls had a crush on him and had more than once caught sight of their sweet and innocently coquettish smiles. From inside the barbershop, a young man was casually looking at him. He was effeminately delicate and good-looking. His golden hair glistened in the light and his tight shirt clung to his well-proportioned body. He had an extraordinarily narrow waist. Mr. Alpha took one more look at his own reflected image, snatched the fur hat off his head, and resumed his walk. As he turned a corner, he examined himself again in a shop window and turned his head in disgust, heading quickly for the next street. Around the corner, he caught sight of the artillery colonel standing next to a telephone booth waiting his turn.

Before he could leave the scene, the colonel saw him and called him over. The colonel had his little girl on his shoulders and was swaying her back-and-forth. Soraya Dilmaghani, the colonel's wife, was standing a little farther away talking to the young student Mr. Alpha knew from before. The line at the phone booth was long and composed of Arabs, blacks, and some other foreign types.

"This phone is out of order," said the colonel. "It doesn't pass the coins. You could call anywhere free. You can talk as long as you want."

Mrs. Dilmaghani gave a faint smile and shook Mr. Alpha's hand limply. She then gave a sad, unexpected laugh. Her clothing was unseasonably light, and she shivered incessantly. The young man did not acknowledge Mr. Alpha. Obviously, he had no intention of returning the money he had borrowed from him

A police car drove slowly past, and a visible ripple of anxiety went through the line of callers. By now, a few more people had learned about the malfunctioning apparatus and had joined the line.

A soft drizzle had begun to fall. Soraya Dilmaghani was definitely feeling cold. She coughed and said, "To hell with this life." She nervously brushed her peroxide blond hair. She was a basically beautiful woman, young and subdued.

Now the Colonel's turn had come to use the phone. He stepped inside the booth and dialed a number, evidently of his brother. He was on the phone a long time. He also talked to his mother. There was much protest in the waiting line, but the colonel turned a deaf ear to it and dialed another number, handing the phone to his wife who cried profusely throughout the conversation. She then gave the phone back to her husband, eyes still streaming. "I'm going back," she sobbed. "Damn Paris, its climate, and its people. I'm going back." The colonel was still in the booth. The student, in an attempt to mollify her, said, "Thank God you managed to escape that inferno. A nation of diseased, dilapidated, and worthless people! As for me, I'm going to America. That's heaven!"

The Colonel called Mr. Alpha to the booth.

"It's my turn," the student protested.

Mr. Alpha blushed and stepped aside. "Please, go ahead," he said timidly. "I have no one to call."

Mrs. Dilmaghani took refuge from the rain under an awning. She did not have an umbrella or a raincoat. The Colonel took Mr. Alpha by the shoulder and heaved him into the booth. "Man, don't be shy," he admonished Mr. Alpha. "Opportunities like this don't come along often.

Use it!" Mr. Alpha, hesitant and mortified by the loud objections of the people waiting outside, just stood there, receiver in hand. In a harsh tone, the student said he was in a hurry and had to call someone in San Francisco. Compulsively, the colonel gathered his daughter in his arm and gave her a tight hug, which caused the little girl to scream with pain and beat her little fists on her father's nose and mouth. Mr. Alpha was still standing indecisively in the booth, receiver in hand, not knowing what to do. He physically felt everyone's stare on his back. The franc piece was still stuck in the phone. In all these months he had never called Mrs. Nabovat. He had never thought about the reason. Perhaps the cost had been a consideration, but more likely he had no idea what to tell her. Now he could perhaps have five minutes. How could he cram everything he had to say in such a short time? He did not even know how to begin or how to end. His hand holding the receiver began to shake violently. He had to hurry because the crowd outside was getting ugly. He dialed "19" and was connected to the international exchange. He doubted that he should go through with the call. He was now beginning to get used to his circumstance. The sound of Mrs. Nabovat's voice would drive him crazy again and precipitate another attack of nostalgia. He wished he could hang up and get out. But now, the temptation had waxed too potent. He dialed the code for Tehran and got a busy signal. The colonel poked his head in the booth and said, "Never mind. Keep trying." He dialed the international code and then the country and city codes. There was a long pause, and suddenly Tehran came on the line. His ear reverberated with a cacophony of sounds transmitted through the small, grey earpiece from far off, across seas and mountains, from vaguely familiar neighborhoods. An invisible metropolis breathed in his ear and the distant voice of an unknown woman uttered indistinct words. Tehran with all its dusty highways and by-ways, all those friends, acquaintances and students, all the years and the life he had spent in it with his class. The entire continuum of a people's history now was buzzing in his ear.

For one frightening moment, Mr. Alpha thought he had forgotten Mrs. Nabovat's phone number. Frantically, he juggled innumerable digits in his head and could not come up with the right combination. And then he reached for the dial and his finger, guided by the force of habit, touched the number two. His hand had retained its kinetic memory and was automatically dialing Mrs. Nabovat's number!

Mr. Alpha, gripped by excitement and anticipation, felt oppressively hot, and there was a tingling sensation at the tip of his fingers as they touched the dial. It was as if they were touching warm, live flesh, the sensitive points of a naked body. As he dialed the fourth digit, there was a suspicious click followed by a whistling sound. But he was not cut off. By now he had dialed half the digits and could already hear an echo of Mrs. Nabovat's voice. Who would pick up the phone? Mrs. Nabovat? Her husband? Or the cantankerous old housemaid? Certainly, Mrs. Nabovat would answer the phone. She would be so surprised. In her incredulity, she would not recognize his voice. And she would be overcome with anxiety. "Is that you?" she would ask apprehensively. "What's happened? Are you all right?" Then she would immediately think of the money it cost to call from Paris. Mr. Alpha made a mental note to let her know as soon as she picked up the phone that the call was free and they could talk for hours, that as in the past they could laugh and joke about the eccentricities of the principal and Mrs. Cheraghi or Mr. Milani's odd behavior. They could talk, as they used to so often, of the dreams they had had the night before, of sudden toothaches, bilious attacks, current movies, wild rumors, and a thousand other such trivialities, just as they had done for so many years every morning and evening. The colonel was now knocking on the door. "What's the matter? Are you dozing off? Why aren't you talking?" Mr. Alpha resumed dialing. When he got to the seventh digit, unaccountably he had a vivid vision of the Elahieh neighborhood, and the familiar odors of Chenaran Lane pervaded his nostrils. He could clearly see the old mulberry vendor and his donkey passing by Roomi Bridge and his doleful refrain advertising his goods. A bowl of fresh mulberries went for two *rials*, and there again Mr. Alpha saw the sprightly vision of the little girl next door with mulberry stains all over her hands and her face, licking the last dregs of the juice in her bowl. She always had such an insatiable appetite for mulberries. She would eat a whole caskful and playfully raid the other people's bowls.

The last digit in Mrs. Nabovat's phone number was zero. Mr. Alpha's fingertip touched the dial, and an indescribably delicious tremor went through his body. He felt it ripple from his wrists to his thighs. All his thoughts were now concentrated on the tiny dot on the dial, and his senses converged on that magic circle. He felt as if he had his finger on Mrs. Nabovat's navel, the very center of his universe.

By now the dialing was complete. There was a profound silence on the line and then the ringing began. He could see the gray phone on a small table in the entrance hall. He could hear it ringing. He visualized the perennial small vase of flowers next to the phone, Alireza Nabovat's key chain casually lying in the crystal ashtray, a pile of utility bills, a little farther down the hall near the washroom, Mrs. Nabovat's raincoat hanging from a coat rack. Slowly, meticulously, not missing any detail, Mr. Alpha allowed his mind's eye to roam through all downstairs rooms, the kitchen, and pantry, and run hurriedly up the stairs. There, it passed over the beds, making a brief pause over Mrs. Nabovat's hair brush and hand-held mirror, surveying the balcony and the rooftop, brushing lovingly past the wash on the clothes-line, sliding down the wall, desperately swinging through the front yard and peeking up and down the alley. The house was all closed up, dark, and shuttered. The gray phone on the small table in the hall was still ringing.

The Colonel poked his head in the booth and said: "They don't answer?" Mr. Alpha allowed the telephone to ring for the tenth, eleventh, and twelfth times. He then hung up.

"Call someone else," the colonel insisted. "You won't find another free phone."

It was now the student's turn. He bustled his way into the booth and shut the door. The waiting line moved one step forward.

In the cafe, Soraya Dilmaghani had huddled against the wall and was staring at her empty teacup. She was still cold and shivering. Her husband, the Colonel, plumped down on a chair and motioned Mr. Alpha to another. He lifted up the child onto his lap and gave her a hard squeeze. The child shrieked. The Colonel had become a father late in life, and the little girl was his only child.

Mrs. Dilmaghani was hungry. Nervously, she chewed on her nails. Saying that she had had nothing to eat all morning, she got a pill out of her bag and popped it down her throat. The colonel ignored his wife's pronouncements. Mr. Alpha, feeling obligated, ordered a cheese sandwich and an ice-cream for the girl He couldn't help noticing Mrs. Dilmaghani's grateful glance. To relieve his embarrassment, he pointed to the student who was now approaching their table. He got up and rearranged his chair to make room for him. He was trying to convince himself that the young man would pay him back. To divert his thoughts from the matter, he broached the subject of the New Year and the advent of spring. He issued a blanket New Year's felicitation to all present.

With a teaspoon, the colonel took a large dollop from the girl's ice cream and put it in his mouth. The girl hollered in protest.

Soraya Dilmaghani, looking for some reason mortified, cast a furtive glance around the room. The colonel laughed coarsely and repeated his raid on the ice cream and offered some to Mr. Alpha. By this time, the child had slid all the way to the floor and was screaming her head off. The colonel extracted her forcibly from under the table, showering her with effusively affectionate terms.

"This time everything will go right," the student was saying to no one in particular, unperturbed by all the noise. "They're going to send me a work permit. I'm going to America. One hundred percent sure."

Inconspicuously, Soraya Dilmaghani wrapped the uneaten part of the sandwich in a paper napkin and dropped it in her handbag. "I'm going to go back to Iran," she said. "I so miss that land, its sunshine and its folks."

The colonel said, "We will all go back."

Mr. Alpha was still thinking of the gray telephone on the small table. His head was full of echoes of distant sounds.

The student got to his feet and drank the last sip from his coffee. He then said good-bye and moved toward the door. Soraya Dilmaghani, doe-eyed, watched him leave.

Mr. Alpha paid the bill. The colonel, as he carried his daughter in his arms, was telling her in a singsong tone, "My little lady, my sweet candy, I'll take you back to Iran. That's where you'll grow up and learn to be a sweetheart of a gal. That's where you'll marry and be a lady. You'll never have anything to do with France. You're not *la demoiselle* Farideh! You're my girl, the daughter of a colonel in the Imperial Army!"

Soraya Dilmaghani commandeered her husband's raincoat and stepped into the street ahead of the rest. She was looking at the sky and ominous clouds, when she stepped on a pile of dog turds. She was beside herself with rage and frustration. A stream of curses poured out of her mouth as she hung onto her husband's arm. She looked totally despondent, as someone in the throes of a major disaster. In her despair and helplessness she looked at Mr. Alpha for relief.

The colonel for his part uttered a few obscenities at the canine species in general, but it was obvious he was not going to do anything about the situation.

Mr. Alpha, resentful but feeling that he was somehow implicated, gingerly reached for the shoe and extricated it from the offensive matter. As much as it was possible, he cleaned the shoe by scraping it against the curb and wiping it with a paper napkin he produced from his pocket. With as much sympathy as he could muster, he told Mrs. Dilmaghani he was sorry but that was the best he could do. "If I were you," he added, "I'd write this shoe off."

"This is the only decent pair of shoes I've got," protested Mrs. Dilmaghani. "And I brought these from Tehran. The franc has gone up to sixty *rials*. A pair of shoes would cost a fortune. We'll soon have to walk barefoot, I suppose."

Mr. Alpha decided to part company. "Good-bye, dear sir," the colonel said. "We'll see each other soon, I trust. We are more or less homeless these days and we have to impose on someone everyday. Who knows? We may be knocking on your door before long."

"You will be most welcome," said Mr. Alpha, hurriedly walking away. As he passed the phone booth, he noticed a repairman was working on it.

By the time Mr. Alpha reached his own neighborhood, it was late afternoon. The rain had stopped and the public garden looked fresher and greener than usual. Birds were perched on branches so motionless they looked as if they were carved out of stone.

151

Mr. Alpha took a bag of breadcrumbs out of his pocket and stopped in the park. He sat on a bench after he carefully dried it with a handkerchief. The pigeons opened their eyes and turned their heads towards him. Mr. Alpha sprinkled some crumbs at his feet and some on his head and shoulders. "These are now my students, the bards of my bower," he thought to himself, as he relaxed and dropped his hands to his sides. He had given names to the birds by which he identified them: Lady Pigeon, Lazy Pigeon, Bright Pigeon, Polite Pigeon, etc. He called the roll every time he fed them. He even gave them grades and talked to them.

Half-drunk and oblivious to her surroundings, an old beggar woman walked past the far end of the park, singing off-key.

Pigeons started cooing and fidgeting uncertainly. "My dear ones, please listen," said Mr. Alpha, addressing the birds. "This is a history class. Today we have an examination."

A pigeon flew a half circle and landed at Mr. Alpha's feet. It cautiously pecked at a piece of bread and scampered back. Other pigeons craned their necks and flew down to the grass en masse. Dreamily, Mr. Alpha admonished them to observe order. "Write this down," said he, allowing authority to creep into his voice. "Question Number One."

The birds, now unafraid, were in flurry of feeding on the crumbs. One of them had lighted on Mr. Alpha's pate, the tip of its tale brushing his face. Mr. Alpha could sense the animal odor and warmth radiating from its body. The smell was pleasant, that of a bird hatching an egg. Another pigeon was in his lap pecking at his fly. He had a strong sense of the collective warmth and breath of the young birds gathered around him, and the affection he felt for them flooded his heart. He reached for a bird, and it submitted trustingly to his touch. He stroked its head and back as he held it gently. He then let it fly off. By now the birds were all over him, jostling on his shoulders, on his head, and the palms of his hands.

It was such a serene evening. The air was redolent with the fragrance of spring exuding from the surrounding greenery. There was an amorphous vitality in the air, which was on its way to take shape and give form to the times to come.

Mr. Alpha leaned his head on the back of the bench and stretched his legs. A beatific mood contorted his body and he wished he could prolong the feeling indefinitely. He wished he could sit there for the rest of his days and let the pigeons nestle on his eyes and lips and raise their young in his hair and with him review all the chapters of history.

In his reverie, Mr. Alpha was transported to an erstwhile exam session in a sophomore high-school class. "Write this down," he intoned. "First question: Alexander's invasion of Persia and the fall of the Achaemenid dynasty."

The weather was changing from moment to moment. The rain was about to let loose again. There was a rustling sound in the surrounding bushes. Mr. Alpha could not determine its source. He opened his umbrella when a few large raindrops fell on his face, but did not get up. He felt good and his heart, now feeling strangely boyish despite his fifty-two years, was laden with a vague anticipation of good news. Mr. Alpha was reminded of the sentence in Mrs. Nabovat's letter: "Keep your door open, dear. Perhaps seeing Khezr will fall to your lot."

Rain in Europe was nothing like the welcome light drizzles in Tehran; it came down in persistent torrents. The birds had now taken refuge from the rain under the eaves of nearby buildings. Mr. Alpha, like someone mildly inebriated, was chanting a familiar strain: "Temptation is in the air and airy-headed am I!" Deep inside his head Mr. Alpha could feel a sweet tingling vibration. It was Mrs. Nabovat's whistle, eternally echoing from those distant spring days to this.

The park attendant in the small guardhouse was looking in Mr. Alpha's general direction. Remembering that he did not have his passport on him and that his residence permit had expired, Mr. Alpha felt uneasy. He lowered his umbrella to shield his face. He glanced at his new shoes, which by now were soaking wet. Alireza Nabovat had sent him these shoes from Tehran.

Mr. Alpha rose to his feet and stuffed the bag of breadcrumbs in his pocket. Under the eaves, the pigeons appeared to him in a somber mood. Perhaps they were contemplating migration to another land.

He thought he recognized the barking of a dog that belonged to the concierge. Mr. Alpha looked around him, dazed and disoriented, wondering, "What the hell am I doing in this place?" He started feeling that false hunger, that cold emptiness circulating in his bowels again, causing him to feel nauseous. He felt he was at the tail end of a strange dream that had frightened him. "No, this place is not for me," he muttered to himself. "This is not my kind of town. I'll head home tomorrow. Or next week at the first opportunity."

He felt soothed by this decision as he entered the apartment house. He shook his umbrella vigorously so it wouldn't drip on the staircase and cause further trouble. He then put the cigarette butt in his coat pocket and cautiously rounded the corner in the hallway. After he entered his room, he closed the door noiselessly behind him and heaved a deep sigh of relief.

---

[1] God is great.

[2] Obligatory prayer that is performed five times a day.

[3] A Shi'ite holy day mourning the martyrdom of Imam Hussein.

[4] The Omayyad governor of the region at the time of Hussein's insurrection.

[5] A combination of an Iranian mythical personage and Elijah, the prominent figure in the Old Testament. In the Iranian folk tradition, he is the holder of the key to heavenly bliss.